Two Tales

Family Portrait

A Woman's Man

Margaret Buckley

The Chrysalis Press

First edition 1993
(first issue of 350 copies)

by The Chrysalis Press
11 Convent Close, Kenilworth, Warwickshire

British Library Cataloguing in Publication Data:
Buckley, Margaret (1930-1992)
Two Tales: Family Portrait & A Woman's Man
I. Title F

ISBN 1 897765 01 0

Two Tales

By the same author

The Commune

With Brian Buckley

Challenge & Renewal: Lawrence and the Thematic Novel

Available from the Chrysalis Press

FAMILY PORTRAIT

1

Louise stood adjusting the shawl round her baby's face waiting for her husband to finish fiddling in his pocket for the key and get the street door open, but before he managed it the door sprung wide and his younger brother Mike stood on the step radiant with smiles waiting for the moment to express his feelings. It took too long. Coming out and flinging his arms round Louise and the baby together he squeezed till she forced a way out with her elbows:

"Watch out, you'll squash her!"

Mike's slight body and excited brown eyes still offered themselves after the rebuff.

She smiled affectionately. "Out of the way - let's see Mum." She was moving past him into the house.

Mum was Louise's mother-in-law. Increased noise in the kitchen announced where she was and Louise knew Ruth would wait for them to come to her. Straightening her back, smiling and triumphant she opened the door, to be met by Ruth's back.

Ruth suddenly turned saying, "There you are then!" Her instant precedence was backed by the way she moved and looked. She was suppressing excitement. "Let's have a look at her." She pulled the shawl away. "Ah!" - she was amused - "just like Grandmother Sharp," she said, "you'll have your work cut out!" Louise studied her daughter's face carefully. "Go in and I'll bring some sandwiches."

Mike followed Louise into the sittingroom hovering close and standing behind her when she sat. He muttered in her ear, "I've bought you a cake," and reached his hand round to touch the baby's face and hide his affection.

Louise was tremendously elated. She was home in a new capacity and full of the power she'd been waiting for. Looking at the cake with Congratulations Mother iced in red she nestled her rosy face against her daughter and looked up to see Ruth holding out a plate of sandwiches and cup of tea. She put them by Louise's side and reached for the baby.

"No, you'll wake her, let her sleep. She's such a crier."

"I'd like a closer look." Ruth was peremptory and speaking to Harry who reached to take his daughter.

"I said no!" Louise shuffled the child dexterously to one side freeing her right hand. "Now, if you'll pass a sandwich." Harry passed the plate. "Just a sandwich, I can't manage both."

He handed it to her with an irritated glance.

They were silent while she ate and sipped her tea. Her new power felt limitless and her eyes blazed at the men sitting opposite staring. Michael's nervous movements as he handed her a piece of his cake filled her with joy. Ruth was going about her business taking no offence. Louise's expression of inviolable possession went unchallenged. They were invited to admire from a distance and Michael, ever responsive, came to crouch in front of her and stare.

"She's so pretty! Look at the powerful chin!"

Louise did - with the pride of having designed it herself.

This baby was perfect!

Harry started getting home earlier to play with his daughter before she was put to bed. The gate between the two gardens (Ruth and Michael lived next door) was always open and they popped in as they felt like it - for Michael this was every day. In the bright evenings Harry rolled about with Molly on the back lawn receiving fat fists full of grass in his mouth and eyes and up his nose - accepting everything for the pleasure of watching her happy and intense curiosity. Michael came home later, had supper with his mother and joined them. Louise sat by amused. Occasionally she was put out by the lengths they'd let the baby go but was more sure of her husband than she'd ever been.

It was the most relaxed period of their marriage. Once or twice an old anxiety came back but didn't stay long. When he was reading in the evenings she'd sometimes find herself observing him closely as she had in the past. If he was deeply involved or his eyes darkened or if he drew in his mouth repressively she'd assume these were erotic passages but nowadays he came out of them his new self. If he was bored he'd stare about him wondering if Molly'd wake up and he could pick her up. If there was nothing doing he'd try to get Louise to talk.

He missed his friend Ted Stokes who'd moved away six months ago. Their talks on politics or things Ted watched on television had kept him going. Now he was left with Louise's short answers and "It's not worth going on about." He never quite gave up:

"There's a fascinating bit in the Science page," he said, putting his Guardian down. "They're certain there's life on other planets - not like ours of course, but they've discovered the same things round some of the nearer planets - same as form the basis of life here."

Louise eventually lifted her eyes from her book. "What things?"

"Gases." He couldn't remember any more. He was excited and didn't want it to go. The facts had been difficult to digest and he decided to generalise rather than give up.

She knew he'd run out of fuel but was still letting off steam. If she asked anything more he'd get confused and the more he lost his grip the more angry and contemptuous he became of her and of the information that seemed to let him down. When he was happy just to let his curiosity float on possibility she could let her own romance float with it. She studied his clothes, his handsome face and whether or not he needed a change of shirt.

He pretended not to notice she wasn't listening.

Fewer evenings left them to themselves as Molly grew older. She was spoilt and active and usually went to bed in such a state of excitement she couldn't sleep. Neither father nor daughter could do without the romps that preceded bedtime and when Louise put an embargo on them Molly lay upstairs crying till one of them came up and played with her. She'd drop off to sleep only from exhaustion and that took longer and longer to reach.

The parents had fierce disagreements as to how to bring her up - rows over diet and what Louise called "forcing." In one of them she pushed Harry off from pouring cold water down the baby's spine while she was in her bath - he'd read it strengthened the back and stimulated the nervous system.

When Molly was two she knew and sang to her coterie many of the pop songs her mother listened to on the radio, disappearing behind a curtain and then presenting herself with "Clap, everybody!" Energetic and affectionate, she had her father's large blue eyes that, like Michael's, earnestly reflected the expressions of others as well as showing her own. Her expressions and manner were the subject of repeated mimicries and only Ruth reserved judgment. Michael could bear to listen for the sixteenth time and with relish to the story of how at eighteen months a bundle of woollies ran with wobbly speed into the legs of a stranger saying, "Solly, Auntie!"

Surrounded by worshippers she was often uneasy. Greedy for challenge in almost any form, enjoying outdoing herself because then her parents wore their happiest faces, she was often fretful and anxious for no apparent reason. "Overdoing it" became part of her nature, so did anxiety and fear.

She felt an easy lordship over her uncle - he was the gentlest and easiest to please - but with her parents she was seldom released, however joyous they were with her. There was often an uneasiness between them that she translated as reservation with herself. She often felt easier with Ruth who was not her subject but her champion. Ruth felt she was a child after her own heart that needed more controlling than she got - even so she didn't always back Louise's scoldings. If Molly ran next door having delivered the ultimatum, "Tell-a-nanny" and received the answer, "Tell her then," she'd get brisk comfort, drinks and biscuits but sometimes, if she were crying, she'd regretfully watch her grandmother's angry face disappear through the garden gate, and cry louder hearing the voices raised from next door, till they came back to release her.

She liked her grandmother's house. It was peaceful and smelt and looked different. The favourite smells were of cat and the dye of the material on the sofa. She liked lying on it to play with the cat who was a little old for fun of her kind. He allowed himself to be heaved on to the couch, his fat stomach and half-asleep body hanging precariously from her grip, and be fondled and teased. A slight narrowing of the eyes or subjection of the ears made comment in an otherwise passive state and he went back to sleep as soon as she let him.

Ruth liked looking after Molly. She didn't make so many demands on her grandmother and Ruth didn't expect so much from her. In this house Molly found the privacy for quiet exploration which could be abandoned as soon as it got boring for the hectic give and take of her relationship with Louise.

If Michael came home when she was in Ruth's house she got as joyous if not as wild a welcome as from her father. Michael recognised in Molly some of the fire he'd loved in Louise - a quick, careless, lively readiness to enjoy anything. The liveliness hadn't been so much in evidence after her marriage but since Molly'd been born at least those periods of depression and gratuitous spitefulness towards himself had gone. He loved and admired his brother but saw that as a couple they'd never get on so well as now.

2

When he had the chance Harry Spalding wandered round the docks where he was a clerk, watching the boats dock and unload. His glimpses were brief - the business of checking a bill of lading or arguing priorities with the foreman took most of his attention but his interest was always in the ships. The careless banging of a door, sudden shouts and bustle on board, black oily water slapping the hull, paint-stripped handrails, worn gangplanks, a dusty smell of grain unloading and he had a picture of life at sea no closer observation ever damaged, one where small anxieties were lost in travel and land-diminishing oceans. Taking part for short spells in the routine of a place like Port Said or Bangkok - not in the insulated role of a tourist but having a working right to be there - seemed like belonging everywhere rather than somewhere.

When he got home he realised he was glamorising. A more careful scrutiny the next day of some of the faces of the older seamen revealed it clearly and he forced himself to imagine what several weeks cooped up at sea might really be like - practical routines more imperative than in a house, enforced proximity to men, many of whom he wouldn't like - and no privacy. There'd be no real independence, less than in his present job where within limits he decided for himself what to do next. In fact he disliked routines even more than physical and mechanical work. He'd do nothing regularly and if something needed mending in the house he'd avoid it like the plague, knowing how much nervous rather than physical energy it would cost. He seemed never to have the right tools or the right attitudes.

Still the fantasy returned. His cooler self never delayed his going to the dockside on the slightest pretext or the tightening in his stomach and brightening of his eyes. To some extent he followed his enthusiasm in his reading. He was reading more than ever now, especially books by foreign authors. He told himself if a book had been good enough to get translated it must be worthwhile. He'd had repeated evidence it wasn't true but his hand still reached for foreign names on the covers - though stepping up his reading had another cause - it stopped obsessive thinking about his friend's sister Hilda. He'd had time to realise this was based on more than charmed fascination at her sharing his mental world or, for that matter, compassion at her widowhood. He'd had a narrow escape.

The hour or two spent on the bus going to and from work had always been valued reading time, so on the rare trips he shared with Louise he read from habit, which irritated and frustrated her. She had her own sense of adventure going strong and not on paper: shifting around in her seat getting views of the outside - clothes in shops flashing by - an infant wobbling too near the kerb. "Did you see that?" might come out but never got an answer.

Stranded in her reactions, she felt his lack of interest was a judgment on them but when they took Molly it was different. For one thing they went to places with a life of their own, not museums or art galleries. Parks, fairs, zoos were enlivened even for him by Molly's responses and Louise was spared sneers on her choice of place. He was so lively and natural on those days she lost the urge to go places without her. Molly thrived on the trips and her importance. Her parents' eyes full of interest - lives suspended in watching her confronting something new - increased her exposure to it, as if she were the only one it was happening to. It sometimes frightened her.

On one zoo visit they'd been walking round for some time and she'd grown tired and nervous. For the last half hour she'd been carried around on her father's shoulders and had a view of animals over people's heads and over fences. The feeling of direct contact made her hold tight to his neck and chin with one hand while pointing wildly with the other. They went into an enclosed house where the smell alone was too much and came quickly to some railings she couldn't see over. Her eyes followed a yellow-brown column of fur upwards and she bent back her head to follow its loop over the top. The shock of coming face to face with enormous black eyes and flabby lips waving strings of saliva made her scream so loud people came in from outside to see what was wrong. Harry took her down and held her in his arms explaining things. Louise raged silently feeling it was the cold water trick all over again.

One afternoon the three of them went to the local woods to pick bluebells. Louise watched Harry chase Molly through flowers that in patches came up to her middle. Her arms thrust away in front of her, feet pounding through stalks. Harry mimicked her laughter and hid behind trees. Molly, flushed, open-mouthed, bright-eyed waited for the crucial moment, then "Boo!" - and he was looming over her, arms outstretched.

Louise let her vigilance relax. It was a surprisingly warm late Spring day and she took off her coat. Spreading it on the grass she lay on it watching branches lurch and pull back in the light wind. She was warm in the sun and felt drowsy. To Harry relaxing into it wasn't a vital reaction - he was excited and had to be active. For Louise it was a consummate sense of belonging and she was almost asleep when she suddenly realised she couldn't hear Molly and sat up. Anxious and irritated at his leaving her she picked up her coat and went half-heartedly down the path just ahead. She heard voices - a child's among them - and followed the sounds. A few yards to her left she saw Molly's yellow hat bobbing between bushes and as she turned came suddenly up against Harry's half-concealed back. Just beyond him was Hilda Stokes.

The shock of recognition was too sudden to control. Turning pale she clutched at his coat screwing it under her fingers. The Swedish-looking woman had changed since she saw her last. She looked younger than thirty-one and had grown her hair long, it was loose round her shoulders.

Harry, tense, took his wife's hand to stop her dragging at his jacket. She didn't look at Hilda who was addressing her but at the pupils of his eyes contracted to little points.

Hilda was now holding out her hand towards her and Louise stared at it. Hilda looked to Harry for help.

"She's taken a flat near here," he said, "and the children stay with their grandmother after school. She's training at the local college to be a teacher - two year course, isn't it?"

"Yes," she told Louise. "Since Bob died I've had to do something - find a job that took up my interest and paid enough. Teaching's perfect - I'll be free when the children are."

Harry looked at her with respect.

Oh Christ, oh Christ! - the panic in Louise's head turned suddenly to anger and caught between both she couldn't answer. When words came out they were stumbling: "Excuse me - it was a shock seeing you - I fell asleep back there" - she looked at Harry - "I'm feeling ill."

Harry wasn't ready to move.

A whine crept into her voice: "My tummy - since Molly's birth it's very tricky." She looked so pale Harry was worried. He put his arm round her and tears trickled down her face. She was looking at Hilda and Hilda at her. "It's been nice to see you again," she said.

"Yes, hasn't it," Harry added, "she must come round to tea, mustn't she? - say next Sunday? Bring the kids."

"I'll look forward to it." Hilda shook his hand smiling into his face.

Through all this Molly'd been holding on to the back of her mother's dress. She'd set up a quiet anxious whimpering no-one noticed. On the way back Harry threw her up on his shoulders but she wasn't appeased.

Louise was cross with her: "Shut up, can't you!" Molly cried louder.

"Don't take it out on her!" Harry reached her down carrying her in his arms.

"There's nothing wrong with her, it's me who's ill!"

"You're not a baby - you just act like one!"

She clenched her jaw and stopped walking. Harry went ahead comforting Molly. Louise followed at a distance in her own time.

By the time Molly got to sleep that night they were both so tired they'd convinced themselves there was no point talking. Harry decided there'd been nothing physically wrong with Louise. She'd stopped complaining when she got home.

"Go to bed," he said, "you look washed out."

In the morning Louise woke with her arm round her husband. When the previous day came back to her she drove it away - warmth and contact were all that mattered - nothing was real outside it.

While Harry was at work and Molly sitting at the table trying to make a cardboard castle Louise stared over her daughter's head at her line of sheets and pillowcases billowing in the wind. She'd never felt happier.

3

The following Sunday Louise seemed abstracted rather than anxious. She hardly spoke to Harry or noticed Molly - so Molly was sulky and tearful - but there were no signs of the fear that had overcome her in the woods. It was Harry who looked anxious. Pale and tight-faced, he was more difficult to reach than Louise and what little success Molly achieved she didn't like: talking, clamouring, upsetting the bucket of water he was using to clean the windows she made him irritable.

By 4.30 when the visitors were expected the Spalding family were dressed in their best and the house tidy. Molly was a miserable exhibition piece. Sandwiches and cakes were covered with napkins on the sideboard. The guests arrived on the dot with the two Stokes girls announcing their presence by quarrelling loudly down the front path. Harry opened the door before they'd pressed the bell.

"Hello, hello! How nice to see you." He picked up the youngest who was seven and stiff with embarrassment. He pressed her to him like a log hoping to conceal his spasm of excitement but Hilda had seen it.

Louise appeared behind him. The roundness and pallor of her face were emphasised by the heavy mass of newly-washed black hair hanging loose. She received an affable handshake. Hilda noticed with slight alarm that Louise was looking particularly nice, but her expression or lack of it - a blank, shuttered look - spoilt the effect. Now she felt ready to do what she'd come for.

They went single file to the sittingroom which felt far too small. The children stood waiting for directions. Molly stared relentlessly at Janine who seeming not to notice drew closer to her older sister who was making no commitment to anyone.

Harry suddenly exploded with high spirits: "We can't stand around like this, let's get some more space - good thing the weather's fine!" - and unbolting the French windows fixed them wide with two bricks. "Out you go, kids - plenty of room in the garden!"

"Go on, Sally, take Janine out - have a go on the swing." Hilda pushed her shoulder and the ten-year-old went like a robot. Janine followed.

Molly stayed where she was looking up at her mother: "Daddy put his dirty fingers on the window, Mummy."

Louise took no notice and sat down. The others followed suit.

"Daddy put his dirty fingers on the window, Mummy!"

"Never mind."

"Daddy said I mustn't put my - "

"Shut up, will you Molly, just for five seconds! Go out and play with the others." Her father picked her up and put her on the lawn.

She stood there. Sally sat on the unmoving swing, Janine leaned against one of the supports, Molly stared into the sittingroom.

Ignoring them Harry said, "Tell us about the college - what are you doing, how do you like it?" He was facing Hilda and crossed his legs.

Hilda glanced at Louise wanting to include her but she was preoccupied with the still life on the lawn. Relief relaxing her voice, "Ah, Harry!" she said, "I'm enjoying it so much I don't want to qualify."

He shuffled forward.

"I never realised I could be so keen. I love reading and

discussing what I read - even love writing about it. I'm beginning to find it's almost all I think about."

Harry sighed. Louise got up and uncovered the sandwiches offering Hilda the plate.

She shook her head. "Not just yet, thanks, I'm not really hungry."

"You're like me, you know" - Harry too was shaking his head at the plate - "I miss the arguments I used to have with Ted" - and a softened, nostalgic look came into his face. Hilda went pink. "I never knew how much I depended on them till he moved. Remember the talk we had on bringing up kids? I'd picked up Rousseau and was full of how the bastard had such good ideas and let his kids die in the workhouse. I remember you said you were going to read it - did you?" The question seemed to challenge their intimacy and she looked disappointed at not being able to give the answer he wanted.

"I'm such a lazy devil. I've only just got into the habit of reading again. Since I've had to it's brought back how good it is." Her eyes appealed for forgiveness and it was granted. Her hand moved a little in her lap as if towards him.

Louise, at Harry's side holding the plate, watched her and turning to see his lifted face and hands pressed together between his thighs put her free hand on his shoulder.

"There's no reason why we shouldn't all meet up again at your flat or here," Harry said, almost unaware of the pressure.

"You could read the books I'm reading at college and we'd talk about them - it would be such a help to me."

Louise stared at the cake still under paper and blocked out their words, only listening to their changing tones, aware of sounds and movements as if they were birds adjusting their balance on the same twig.

14

Harry was pretending to be flustered. "You can't expect a couple of working men to keep up with you."

"You'd manage - you're such a reader. Read the most interesting ones - the ones you fancy."

Louise moved between them. "What about the kids?"

Hilda was confused.

"The kids. Perhaps they'd like to eat. You do it, Harry." She thrust the plate at him.

"Bit early, isn't it? Why me?"

His embarrassed selfconscious look suddenly made her furious and she banged the plate down on the table next to him - a ham sandwich leapt off and sprawled on the floor.

"Because I'm not a bloody servant!" she said.

Silence. After several seconds Harry turned with a white face to Hilda and went on as if nothing had happened. "I'll keep up," he said, but Hilda was pale and looked as if she were about to get up. Harry leaned and touched her knee lightly. "We could meet here Friday evening with Ted and look at your reading lists."

Louise left, slamming the kitchen door so violently the shock jerked Harry into a spontaneous act. He seized Hilda's hand and she stared at it round her own in dazed amazement. Bending towards it she lifted it and put her cheek on the fingers.

They didn't move till Harry saw Molly was standing by him, and disengaged himself. She hauled herself on to his lap by the lapels of his coat and sat studying Hilda. Harry drew her close, rubbing his face on her hair and shutting his eyes. Molly, in total possession, stared. Hilda lurched out of her chair into the garden.

Louise saw from the kitchen Harry was alone and went back, her furious expression changing to a faint smile when she saw the scene in front of her, but she snatched Molly

15

from his knee, the accusation in her eyes keeping him in subjection till with an effort he stood up and joined Hilda on the lawn.

"Let go, let go, Mummy!" - Louise was gripping her too hard and put her down.

"Stay here with Mummy. I'll cut the cake for you, precious - all for you, eh? You shall have the cherry - you shall have the biggest, biggest piece!"

Molly went over to the sideboard and looked proudly at the cake. It seemed a fine idea. She watched the knife go in, watched a triangle of cake with cream on move from side to side as it was loosened and watched it bear away the central cherry. She walked on to the lawn with it in her hand and the other girls came over looking interested.

Hilda was talking, her voice high-pitched and hard. Harry stood close but slightly behind and to one side. She turned when she saw her children move and seeing Louise come out with the cake said, "I was explaining to Harry how daft and depressing some of our tutors are - it's only the course that's exciting."

"They've got their problems," Louise said addressing her for the first time, and Harry looked surprised, even pleased. He went back inside to sit and watch.

Hilda and Louise, stiff, polarised, made movements only towards their children. The Stoke girls were eating and he felt safe for the first time. Molly wandered back to him and hand at the ready he caught her crumbs, deciding there'd be no more meetings at his home.

Louise didn't see Hilda again for a very long time. She knew the three of them met at her flat once a fortnight - it suited her not to know any more. She finally accepted it as she did his Tuesday evening class on home decorating.

4

Molly's schooling stirred a new ingredient into their lives. Both parents were excited and built up an idea of the challenge and adventure so that Molly was keen to go but terrified at the thought of other children, having seldom played in other houses and never in the street. She'd watched small groups from a window but without much interest - the adult world seemed more fun and more exciting, the need to understand what was going on in it had already become a compulsion. From the few times she'd met with children she'd discovered her equals made no concessions and worse still made fun of her. Intensity in her play or in general curiosity put her at a disadvantage. She wanted too much from games, carried things too far, got too excited. They were intrigued but not sure. Part of them backed away as if there were something wrong with her, and it frightened her.

She visited the school with Louise and in a riot of panics took in the hordes of children and the strangers in command. The night before her first school day she sat on the floor next to the dog Harry had given her for her last birthday. She didn't go to meet him when he came home but leant her head against Kim who turned to lick her face keeping his chest squared to the fire. Her father put his hands under her armpits and lifted but she wouldn't come up.

"What's the matter, my sweetheart?" She wished she were Kim, she said. He hauled her up laughing and cuddling her and she ate supper from his fork, sitting on his lap. The next day she was so intensely involved with the new experience she forgot to say goodbye to Louise. For the following week they got little information out of her - she preferred Kim's company.

More than anything else she found it was the routine that worried her. The children quickly understood she was a loner and on the whole left her that way. Her own play world and her dreaming were constantly interrupted by less interesting things. Some things were exciting but they were soon over. The dreaming got worse and became so obsessive she lost track of what was going on. Finding the right room, the right cloakroom, or her peg in a forest of knobs - getting into her P.E. clothes fast enough or joining in games in the playground were all torments. In compensation she was beginning to get the name of being a "good girl." It meant she was no trouble - later it meant she could do her work. If the teacher asked them to sit up straight she put so much into it her back ached. When she looked around she saw not many took it literally and some smiled as if she were an idiot. When they were taught to read and write she took some refuge in it. Her teacher spoke to Louise and her parents seemed pleased but it didn't help her relate at school. At playtime she stood with her back against the wall, hands jammed in her pockets, looking longingly at the skipping games, wishing someone would ask her to join in. Sometimes she'd talk to a pale sickly girl who also stood on the fringes but she wasn't keen on her. Daydreaming became so important she'd sometimes wake up to a lesson half way through it without a clue what to do and at such times she wished someone sat next to her in her double desk. "Molly, stop woolgathering!" was a regular shout from her teacher, only occasionally doing any good.

At home life was wilder than ever. As soon as Harry came in the games began. Waiting for tea with the exciting smell of cooking round them Harry might chase her upstairs roaring like a lion or suddenly grab her legs through the bannisters. They played giggling games, starting innocently enough. The format changed each time:

"I brought my knitting home from school today and did three rows. I've lost a stitch."

"What a shame! - what size was it?"

Slow grin

"Have you looked under the sofa?"

Giggles.

"If we can't find it I'll buy you a new one on Saturday." With Molly shrieking and both of them crawling over the floor looking under furniture Kim joined in - snuffing, flattening himself to get under, barking, licking their faces, more confused and manic by the second - till Louise came in furious:

"Get up, you fools! For God's sake, Harry, leave her alone!"

Sometimes Harry read stories the whole evening, overtly to calm her down and get her ready for bed, in fact continuing their fun in a different form. She had a passion for fairy tales, hating anything realistic. Harry found he enjoyed them himself, his lively eyes reflected what was going on, making fear or achievement in them stronger. It was always Harry she wanted to read. Louise's manner and choice of books were wrong. It was another bone of contention between them.

Louise, angry at the exclusiveness, said one evening, "You're *both* a couple of kids" - and to Harry, "You're the bigger!"

When Molly was in bed and she was stacking ironing she told him, "You're wearing her out with all that mucking about. She's getting thinner. She's lost her rosiness."

"That's school! She's dying for some fun when she gets

home." He reached for his paper.

"Well, I wish you and I had more time together. It's not much of a life for me, we're tired out when she goes to bed."

Head buried in his paper, Harry muttered something about her joining in.

"Don't be daft!"

"Well, why not?"

"We can't all go around screaming."

He shrugged.

"Don't you care about her?"

He didn't answer.

"It gets so out of hand."

"Molly needs excitement. It's her nature. There'd be no pleasure in it for me if there weren't for her - it's good for her."

Louise was still hedging, making it difficult for her to relieve her tension without producing more. She'd only half said what she wanted but he'd made it impossible to go on. How did he always manage to seem in the right? She held down her outrage and her next remark came out viciously: "Why can't you let things be natural?"

He bristled instantly. "Natural?" - shoving the paper aside - "natural is listening to that canned muck you've always got on, or reading her books she doesn't like?" Louise blushed. "I'll make sure she grows up nuts if that's the alternative."

If Louise didn't fight back to her satisfaction the tension could go on for days and everyone caught it.

For Molly things got a little better after Harry discovered she liked music. He never lost an opportunity and immediately offered a special treat - she could listen to Swan Lake with him that evening after supper. The extra late bedtime and Harry's tone made her sick with

20

excitement but when the time came she'd worked up a head of steam the music couldn't satisfy and after listening for a bit became restless. Harry was excited but it was focussed on her. She didn't know what he wanted.

"What's going to happen?" she said.

"Listen - " he took her hand and told her the story - "the music tells you everything."

Molly sat quietly then something in it distressed her and gently removing her hand she leant for the biscuit she'd left on the table. Harry grabbed her shoulders and forced her back:

"Listen!"

Angered at the volume and the drama he made of it Louise got up, fetched the biscuit, gave it her and sat down scraping her chair. She hadn't expected his reaction, meaning only to irritate and make a point. His silent rage, barely able to keep the peace he'd insisted on, affected them both.

Molly stared in panic. Louise was pale. Nobody was listening. Looking from one to the other Molly felt it was her fault - if she'd listened nothing would have happened. She hunched over her knees pretending to.

"Look how pale she is!" Louise muttered.

"I like it, I really do, I like it! - " and as she said it Molly felt for the first time some of its exaggerated tensions coinciding with her own, transforming them. She was pleased, released, and brightening looked at Harry: "I do!" she said with conviction.

Harry relaxed a little. "I knew you would". His tone drew her close to him, pushing Louise out. Molly didn't want that. She looked at her mother but couldn't get a smile.

Harry kept the pressure up and for Molly listening became a refuge, then a new world. When he bought a secondhand piano for her to play she was excited. Lessons on Friday after school became the most important ones. On that day the impact of incidents at school was sharper. Her excitement and total involvement made her music teacher's lined, indifferent face irrelevant to the private struggle except when it warmed to a good performance. If things went well she was calmer than usual on the way home and even Louise began to see its value. Holding Louise with one hand and her music case in the other she felt free to enjoy the world.

With both parents convinced, practice times became good for them too. They sometimes came into the front room to sit with her but she didn't want to see their faces and would have preferred to be alone. The sounds and their organisation gave relief and pleasure and had an intimacy and clarity that transformed her nervousness to energy - her parents prevented the chemical change taking place.

One Saturday all three of them were repainting the kitchen walls and Molly's voice came muffled from under the sink: "Can I play instead?"

Nobody answered. Harry, meticulously careful not to go over the edge on to the one blue wall, was also trying to recapture the feeling of pride he'd felt in the previous night's discussion when Hilda'd said his remarks on children had put her lecturer's "highflown nonsense" to shame. He was anxiously eyeing Louise's approach from the opposite direction. Large, energetic careless strokes - she'd never keep the edge clean.

"Be careful when you reach the blue."

"Okay."

There was a pause.

"Watch it! - you nearly got it, you'll have to slow down."

"Doesn't matter, it'll wash off, it's only emulsion."

"We've just done the blue. It's dry but I don't fancy

rubbing it. Keep clear and slow down. There's no hurry, enjoy it!"

"I am enjoying it! I can't fiddle-fart like you."

Molly, painting the unimportant bit under the sink, came out to have a look. Louise seemed to have done most but she liked the look of her father's best, it was brighter with no thin patches. She went to tell Louise she'd missed a bit near the skirting board and her mother dismissed it: "A blind man would like to see it!"

Molly thought it was true and turned to her father whose face had gone pale, with deep lines from cheek to chin. His mouth was drawn together like a badly sewn slit, but it was his furious eyes that made Molly's bowels turn over in wave after wave of panic. She dropped her brush and rushed to the front room, banging back the piano lid. There was silence for a bit while she found her music, then she played - loud, inaccurate, violent. Harry and Louise came in looking enquiringly at each other, his face now more normal, and Molly went mad with exultation.

Soon a family habit was established that Molly played to her parents before going to bed. They exchanged glances Molly interpreted as proud and possessive. They put in requests for their favourite pieces and loved her excited performance. Louise was always her champion and proud of her - "I think it's marvellous, a little girl of your age!"- but Harry always wanted something more. He wanted something from the performance itself and that excited her. If she could please him in this she could almost be free of the need to please in every other way and she sought his comments even when they made her cry.

Louise couldn't understand why she defended him and was hurt at her unfair partiality. Molly wriggled away when Louise tried to comfort her after Harry's criticism, feeling guilty but unable to stop herself - at bedtime she'd hang round Louise's neck trying to make up for it.

All her inspiration came from Harry. If he said, "Don't thump, you can't impress that way," Molly couldn't sleep for shame at her silly showing off. On the other hand, when her playing lit his face, or when once he said he would have thought a certain piece too adult for her to understand she lay restless from happiness and a sense of power and achievement. The word "adult" came back to her every time she tried to sleep, burning her awake with promise.

5

Starting towards the end of her first school year and continuing through the following three Molly caught one illness after another. Having run through all the childish ailments she started on others, catching pneumonia twice. A bed was made up for her between the window and the fire in the sittingroom so she could feel part of the family still.

While recovering from pneumonia she had a visitor she couldn't remember having seen before though there was something familiar about her. She woke from a doze to see a fairhaired woman standing by the fire and looking at her with tender concern.

"Poor, poor little Molly, how are you, dear?"

The woman's long thick hair fell forward when she came to the bed and leaned over, Molly felt it brush her hand and looked up admiringly. It took some moments for her to feel a need to understand the situation and when she did she looked to her mother. Louise was putting a parcel on the floor by the sideboard.

"Mum?"

"Yes, love? Feeling good enough to sit up?"

Molly was already leaning on one elbow and staring palefaced at the parcel. "What's that?"

The woman went over to it. "May I?" she asked Louise and picked it up. "I've brought you a present." Resting it on the bed she unstuck the sellotape and Molly joined in with trembling fingers. They reached the box and Hilda stood back. Molly went for the tissue paper with a thumping heart and found a doll with long blonde hair and eyes that clicked open, brilliant blue. She was speechless, turning it round, studying the shiny blue dress and silver shoes. She looked up hesitantly.

"For me?"

"Yes, do you like it?"

She looked haggard with excitement. Louise came to prop the pillows behind her but she sprang forward.

"No, lie back, there's a good girl, I'll put the doll by you."

Lying back she felt excused from having to thank the woman as much as she thought she deserved and looked up with gleaming eyes to say "Thanks."

"That's all right, darling." The woman kissed her forehead.

"Hilda's come to wish you better." Louise's tone was clipped, her face tireder than usual.

Molly wondered if she should know her and studied her carefully but the look of deep compassion and the likelihood of a tearful embrace made her turn away, pick up the doll and make an affectionate barrier of it.

"Nice of Hilda to give you that lovely present," Louise said, but the tone upset Molly and she blushed - it was aggressive and seemed to mean the opposite. Embarrassment was too much for her and tears trickled down her cheeks. She wanted the doll more than ever.

Ignoring Louise's manner Hilda leant over again but Louise's arm got in the way tidying the sheet. The visitor moved to the door and turned to wave and as soon as she was alone Molly grabbed the doll and fell asleep.

She woke to find Harry sitting on the bed asking Kim what kind of day he'd had and if he felt better. Kim put his paws in Harry's hands and danced about on his back legs.

"Poor Kim!" Molly instantly joined in. The dog's eyes looked anxious and gleeful in turns. Molly sat up and took a paw from her father. "Poor old pink-belly - are you better then?" Front paws stretched, he leapt up and down to get on to the bed, his back paws scraping the blanket every time he failed.

"Let him down, you silly pair - look what you're doing!" Louise released him and helped Molly sit up.

Looking on the bed and round the room Molly glanced enquiringly at Louise but her anxious eyes and tight mouth prevented asking about the doll. Again she wanted to cry but covered it by being unusually responsive to Harry's fun.

"She's getting better," Harry said, "we're getting our girl back," and got off the bed in great spirits. "Want a bite of tea, my darling?"

Molly shook her head and within minutes was asleep. Later when she woke and Harry was next door with his mother she asked for the doll. It was brought in its box that now had brown wrapping paper loosely round it. She took it out and this time found the eyes too glassy. Its fixed expression irritated her. She asked for a comb and hated the noise it made on its hollow head. Putting it aside she said, "Nice of the lady to buy me that."

"Mmm." Louise was preparing to knit and sat with her back to her. "Do you want to listen to the radio for a bit?"

"No." Molly thought before asking the next question: "Who is she? She's got such pretty hair."

When Louise turned Molly saw she was blushing and getting up to push her back on her pillows. "God, how easy it is! Perhaps you'd like her for your mother?"

Molly repeated her frantic denials the more her memory of the pretty, compassionate face contrasted with Louise's tense and angry one. She lay back and watched her mother knit. "Take the doll away Mum, I want to go to sleep." Louise dumped it in the chair by the fire. "I'm too old for dolls. Stupid of her not to know that." She shut her eyes and fell asleep.

Louise watched her sleeping - the sunken cheeks and dark eyelids releasing an anguish of compassion. She gripped her hands in her lap rocking forwards and back, biting her lip. Tears were pointless - wasted her energy. Harry was free - did as he liked - coddled by his mother at this very moment and she brought out the worst in him. When he came in he'd act like God Almighty. With a spasm of shame she remembered showing Ruth the doll:

"Look at this," she'd said, uneasy at making further comment.

"Who's it from?"

"Hilda - Harry's friend's sister."

Ruth's eyes brightened. "Expensive gift!" she'd said. It was enough.

Still smarting Louise got to her feet and when Harry came back she was polishing the furniture - his chair had been moved and the table pulled out. Mildly complaining he went back to his mother's.

Molly woke next day very late and lay for a long time looking out of the window. She hadn't moved but felt her mother in the room. The sun on the bricks of the shed opposite showed rough pits and blends of red and brown and it shone hard on the blazing roof tiles. Kim was sitting on the concrete apron in front of the French windows - nose moving, tracing a scent. He heaved off and came back a few seconds later to sit in the same place facing the sun, back legs spread, thinskinned belly wide to it. He shut his eyes. Molly's eyes kept turning to the roof.

Louise hadn't been surprised that Hilda knew of Molly's illness - Harry'd be certain to have talked of it - and not surprised at her turning up. It was her manner of deep concern, as if she loved her, that shocked - almost as if Molly'd been her child - and the intimacy producing it terrified her.

She couldn't face going back to the old way of life when Molly got better, she'd take a job - perhaps a course at the local college like Hilda. She started up right now in a small way watching Ruth's television in the mornings for schools programmes and in the evenings not knitting but quietly mulling things over. It bothered Harry but he assumed she was recovering from months of strain.

One evening, fascinated by his white rather plump fingers round the spine of his book, she remembered holding his hand on walks in the early days and not being able to let it go - hardly let him use it for climbing stiles, there was such peace and assurance in the soft grip. Sexual excitement, bewilderingly unreliable, had been replaced by the wealth of contact she could get from cuddling and holding hands - something they never did now. Harry'd quickly sensed her uneasiness with sex and his own appetite abated but as his sexual demands lessened the moral ones increased. When he felt she'd spoken or acted in a way conflicting with his sense of right he felt free to bully her and feel superior doing it since these were issues unrelated to himself. He handled her delicately but she fought back savagely. The more delicate he was the cruder she became - she identified his approach with dishonesty and went so far the other way he had the evidence he needed that she was a bad-natured inferior. She didn't dare tell the truth even if she'd been clear about it - she didn't trust him. His head was crammed with notions. Explaining her problem inadequately would give him a chance to call her frigid - in any case anger at his insensitivity got in the way. Nothing real was safe with him - everything was a 'cause'.

If she challenged him about Hilda he'd be capable not just of admitting to his feelings but of pushing them further to prove a point. She pictured his white face entrenched in a would-be moral position forcing her to face facts. Suppose it wasn't a fact? Suppose he wasn't much involved with Hilda? Making an issue of it would be all he needed. Leave him alone - let him do it in imagination.

Louise had her small square-shaped fists clenched in her lap and her preoccupation was so intense Harry wanted to break into it:

"Everything okay?"

She looked up without answering.

"What you thinking about?"

"Nothing."

"That's not true."

"Nothing important - I was thinking of the programme I saw on kid's telly this morning."

He closed his book, surprised and pleased.

She raked her memory for something to say. "I got quite

29

cross really."

"Why?"

"It was about the human nervous system and brain - but only for young children - reflex actions and so on - it made a lot of how much bigger human brains were."

"What made you cross?"

"They were saying that's why we're more successful - but there aren't more people than fish or birds, are there?"

Harry grinned. "That's not what he meant."

"No, but he should have."

"He means we're capable of more complex lives - of achieving more - "

"More what? - fish and birds have adapted as well as us - that means they've achieved as much." Harry was only half amused. "I'm not carping, but listen. He had this dog there and some steps up to a little platform. To show the kids how dim animals are by comparison (he'd already said they didn't learn but were trainable - as if we weren't) he told this dog several times to climb the steps and of course it didn't. Then he said the dog would do it if you took him to the front of the steps and encouraged him up the way he'd been trained, and so some woman came along and did this and up he went."

Harry wondered if she hadn't understood at this simple level and crossed his legs, waggling his foot. She knew the sign and was discouraged but desperate to show she had a point. When she started up again her mouth was dry and her eyes aggressive.

"Well, what's the point of *telling* him to go up the steps? He would have looked a right fool if the dog had barked some orders to him. I mean dogs have probably got used to people's stupidity and inability to learn."

"You must remember the programme was for young

children. They were trying to get an understanding across at a simple level."

"Yes, but the wrong understanding."

"Was it?"

"That blooming dog would have got up those steps fast enough if there'd been meat at the top. That's intelligence - finding a way to get what you want - not muck-arsing around with meaningless games. It's people who are good at that. The dog showed more sense than the teacher!" She paused. "Watch old Kim's eyes. He imitates our expressions - yearning when he wants to go out or that soft look when you stroke his head. I bet you wouldn't recognise a wild dog's expressions that easily - Kim's learnt all *our* ways. In the wild their ways of communicating wouldn't have anything to do with ours. *You'd* be the one who couldn't learn - but you'd be trainable if your life depended on it."

"He meant animals are not so complicated."

"How do you know? I'd rather watch that bright, shiny-coated, gentle-tempered dog than the dried-up blockhead introducing him!"

"Maybe, but the complexity of people exposes them to more strains."

"Well, if they can't resolve them without destroying their wits and their looks they're *not* successful. The man's sloppy assumptions made me cross. If the dog looks happy and alive he's adjusted to *his* strains."

For once Harry couldn't understand what was going on between them. "What's got into you, Louise? You don't seriously think animals are as complicated as people?"

"Aren't all our problems of the same kind, Harry? We've broken the basics into fragments so there's more bits to worry about - is that anything to boast about? - especially as we're so dishonest about what we really care about. We all need the same things which include communication and acceptance."

"Can't you see what more we need?" He was screwing up his face.

"Not really."

"Achievement, exploration, it's our endless curiosity and creativity makes the difference!"

"But *they're* the same!" His anger had shaken her - the old patterns were re-establishing themselves and she couldn't push ahead.

"The basics aren't enough for us - never have been from the beginning," he said.

Her eyes filled with tears and she blushed not because he'd made his point but because struggling to be on his wavelength had made matters worse. They were so different. Nothing would ever change it and unless he accepted her as she was nothing could change between them. Tears rolled down her cheeks.

Harry romped home: "Don't *you* ever aspire, don't *you* ever want to live more fully than you do?" He stood up, his book fell to the floor and he left the room. Minutes later Louise heard the street door slam. The raised voices and banging door woke Molly. Louise comforted her, fetched a hot drink and sat by the side of her bed. She stroked Molly's head gently and rhythmically and the soothing had a similar effect on herself.

Harry was walking fast along the local streets hating everything. Small ridiculous houses, stupidly neat front gardens, no space, no adventure, no room to move or think! He walked till exhaustion slowed him down. Resentment against the whole bear-trap of houses and marriage worked itself out and he began to think of work on Monday and Hilda on Friday. He turned back. Hilda and he were taking a whole day off together! His spirits were soaring and his hands trembling as he put his key in the front door.

6

Harry'd had a zest for work over the last year and fancied there was a growing dependence in the department on his small acts of self-reliance. The other week there'd been no official customs clearance for some crates of frozen food and to push it through normal channels would have taken too long - the refrigerated lorries were lined up and waiting and had all but reached their limit. He made some phone calls and sent a lad to the customs office on a motorbike. Official side completed, the crates were unloaded and carted off as if there'd been no slip. Working on his own excited him, so did the race against time. By the time his boss got to know it was a fait accompli and his high-handedness earned no gratitude but for Harry it was an unqualified success. The captain was grateful (he'd been threatening to dump the lot on the quayside) and so was the cargo owner who'd been on and off the phone all day.

It was the unexpected that made his clerk's job bearable. If he knew a piece of work was tricky he made sure he was in the middle of it and the others were pleased to let him. If things went wrong he took the can back happily. His manner implied the mess wasn't serious or insoluble but exciting and it had a good effect on the others.

When work was slack Harry liked talking to the two he worked closest with, Ted and Peter. Politics mostly - full of heat and prejudice. Ted set himself up against the quiet unassertive Peter whose middle-of-the-road views made him a target for both sides. Harry leapt in and out wherever he thought he could make a point. He felt like an unofficial chairman preventing discussions from deteriorating into mud-slinging. It linked with his notion of himself as custodian of principle and the common sense of any situation. Louise told him, "Tongue's your favourite dish" but on these occasions he felt he just stood by with the salt and pepper.

He'd kept himself busy this week and by Friday was so 'high' Louise misread the physical symptoms. If it hadn't been for his bright eyes she'd have argued to keep him home. He'd been strange, remote, clumsy about the house and spilt tea down his trousers, forcing him to wear his best suit.

In her bed-sit Hilda Stokes was just as nervous. She'd spent a wakeful night, full of dreams and half-conscious imaginings and got up too early, tireder than when she'd gone to bed. Studying her face in the mirror over the sink she saw bags and dark smudges under the eyes that emphasised her age and she crawled back to bed disgusted. When eventually it was time to dress and make up it was an impersonal business but she found herself making comparisons with other mature students and finding more brightness in her eye and bounce in her manner. The emphasis on youth in her mind was never questioned. The situation she found herself in was for her an expression of it and sometimes satisfactory as such - at others a nuisance taking its time going away.

She'd been twenty-four when Bob died and as normal feelings came back had fought them. In determined attempts to escape she'd loosened her hold on the children and was becoming unreachable when she'd first met Harry.

Ted and he regularly had lunch together and she'd joined them. He'd seemed the perfect distraction - lively, entertaining and no threat. Chatting had become a way of expressing thoughts and feelings she'd never released. He was curious in a refreshingly impersonal way and she looked forward to meeting him. In the afternoons after she'd seen him she was more responsive to her children - which to her justified the return to normality. If he talked about the future, the universe, the adventure of life, his excitement affected her as her children's did. On his part he'd found the perfect listener who responded to his flights of fancy and was excited by whatever excited him.

After a while Harry had been transferred to a different part of the docks and lost touch with them. When he was sent back he renewed his old friendship with Ted but made no more than polite enquiries about Hilda. Ted lived further away so there were no chats after office hours.

The upsurge of feeling in the wood had taken them both by surprise and afterwards for several days Hilda had found herself in a joyous weepy state. She was full of gratitude, having thought she'd never feel like that again. The meetings they'd arranged at her flat with Ted became assignations. Whenever they were alone their frenzied embraces, forced by secrecy to a pitch of intensity they'd never felt before, made them feel this was something to be taken very seriously. Hilda grew afraid of losing him through such fierce desire. His needs were slanted differently.

When they met at Hampstead Station only desire was evident. Her shining eyes, grinning face and abnormal energy scared him and for a while he couldn't talk to her. She noticed only a fresh boyish look and a diffidence of manner that went well with it. He tucked her arm under his and she, suddenly heavy with craving, seemed to hang on to him. He found himself wishing for the brilliance he'd disliked earlier. They looked for an isolated place on the town grass and spread their coats.

"At last!" he said - it was almost irritable. Hilda smiled. His jarring tone was instantly absorbed in the gentle indomitable craving. Harry was amazed at her passivity. Things were different.

She lay back looking at his neck and brown hair, conscious of the smell and warmth of his body.

"You look idiotically happy!" he said and again the tone made her uneasy but he was putting his hand to her face in a gesture of tenderness. He gave her a playful slap on the thigh as he turned, meaning to be intimate but in fact waking her from her trance.

When contact had been limited most of the excitement was released in talk. He wanted that back. "Did I tell you some fool thrush built a nest in our rose bush?" he said. She was surprised but knew the nervousness behind it. "It wasn't strong enough to support a nestful of chicks with her plonking down on it every few minutes and when she landed after a storm she tipped them out. Two were left hanging on thorns."

His look of despairing rage told her everything. She came out of the shock not only as cool and uninterested as he was but full of contempt. She stood up to put on her coat, he stood up with her, relieved. They started back - conscious now of the sad appearance of the Heath and the feel of the grass like soft asphalt.

He couldn't stand it and stopped suddenly to kiss her. "What've I done?"

She was silent.

"Talk to me, I don't know what I'm doing."

She took in the anxiety and unhappiness. "If I tell you,

you must listen and not panic. I'm not going to be hurt again, my feelings are strong but can swing both ways."

He looked puzzled.

"You're not like me. Our situations are different." She paused, thinking how to say it. "For me the relationship has become an obsession. I relive everything when I'm on my own. I can hardly bear distraction in the form of work or the children." It was a relief telling him. "But there's nothing in it to frighten you. For myself I've recently wondered if something like this might be the unbalancing factor in a difficult life - wondered if the stories of suicide through passion had some basis in fact - but I should have known myself better - hurt me enough and the whole thing dies. It's happening now." She withdrew the hand he'd taken, biting back her anger.

He didn't dare speak. They walked for nearly an hour in silence, ending up outside Hilda's flat.

"Looks as if the decision's already been made," he said. He put his arms round her and kissed her and she wanted it. All consciousness was at last in their bodies and their only objective to satisfy them.

7

Half an hour before they met Louise had a phone call. One of Harry's colleagues flustered at not being able to find a bill of lading told her he thought Harry'd been taking care of it: "Could you ask him where it is? If he's not too ill perhaps he'd come to the phone" - and when the silence went on too long said it all again, apologising.

Louise, slowly surfacing, answered suddenly, "I don't know anything about it." For a moment he thought she was going to ring off when she said in a rush, "The flu's got worse. I can't help you, I'm waiting for the doctor," and put the receiver down. She held it there in case it leapt into action - the pressure momentarily squashed the panic and bewilderment she was struggling not to understand. She went to the sittingroom to sit with Molly who was home with a cold and working a jigsaw puzzle.

"Who was that?" Molly asked, knocking the puzzle lid on the floor.

Louise picked it up and stood behind her. "How's it coming on?" She turned the lid over to see the picture. "That's good! - you've got the horse already. Shall I help?" - but she made no attempt and put her hands on Molly's shoulders. "Molly love, I've got to go out for a few minutes, I'll send Gran to sit with you." She kissed her on the back of the head. "Stay in the warm!"

On her way through the garden she prepared herself. Ruth made objections but Louise insisted she needed a prescription - she felt she had flu coming on - and muttering something about hypochondriacs Ruth followed her back. She hated her routine to be interrupted. Since Mike had moved to share rooms with a friend she'd made a fortress of her timetable. Mike needed more freedom to entertain his girlfriend Rose, he'd told Louise, but his rooms were only a short bus ride away and it was Mike who had the flu and it was to him Louise was hurrying.

On the bus she sat holding her handbag tight, conscious of people round her, moving up for a passenger, tucking her coat under her - only aware of practicalities - watching for her stop. She was first off the bus making a dash through the traffic and running down Broadbent Road. Her feelings were beginning to shape. The shuddering churning in her bowels she'd half converted into a yearning for Michael and when she reached his house she knocked imperiously. Another tenant answered.

The urge to throw herself into his arms once she was in his room was frustrated by seeing him in bed. Pale, fed up, lying on his side with a book propped against the back of a chair, his surprised "Lou-lou!" made her start crying. She sat on the bed then flung herself over him.

"What's all this?" he said gently pushing her off and getting up. Louise put her hands over her face sobbing while he fumbled with his dressing gown and sat on the bed by her. His head ached viciously.

She told him about the phone call between fierce bouts of crying that released some of her terror. Michael was so distressed he couldn't look at her. She thought he hadn't understood. "He's off, you see! - he's off for the day with her!" He sat still, looking at his knees. "He's off with Hilda - the one he sees on Fridays - that lost her husband."

Michael had met Hilda and disliked her and was building up a sullen anger against his brother. He put his hand on Louise's thigh and began to stroking it slowly.

"He wasn't normal when he left for work this morning. I knew something was up." She took his hand and stilled it and began to cry again. After a moment she wiped her eyes and nose and held his hot hand with both of hers looking at him to see why he didn't say anything. His eyes were full of angry tears and she put his hand to her face, her own tears streaming over it. Thin and small and delicately strong, it filled her with comfort - she turned up the palm kissing it several times then put it back on her wet cheek. Unconsciously she'd always relied on the intimate understanding between them. Harry was the challenge -

Mike was the friend. She studied the black hairs on the back of his fingers and with a sudden flare of sexual desire looked into his face. He was so ill it felt like a blow but underneath was what had always been there for her, love and an inactive sensitivity that he knew unnerved and angered her. She saw the love and confusion and at this moment would have given everything for that sensitivity.

"Come on, my love," she said at last, "get back into bed - you'll get pneumonia or something," and he allowed her to coax off his dressing gown and push him gently back into bed. He lay there, shutting his eyes. "I'm sorry I came - it was all I could think of - coming to see you and crying on your shoulder. I'm sorry - " then suddenly, "don't tell Ruth."

He opened his eyes with a look of love that changed in a moment to the expression both were used to, and said, "You'll be all right, he'll never leave you," adding after a short pause, "Look under the chair - I've done some pictures for Molly."

She found them and rolled them up without looking at them. "Get back to sleep," she said kissing him on the forehead.

On Michael's wedding day Molly lived up to her reputation and was sick three times from excitement. She saw a black car with ribbons drawing up next door and Rose's healthy face surrounded with lace turned towards her. Louise grabbed her arm and dragged her to the bathroom for fear of more joy and Molly was indignant - she couldn't be sick with her dress on. Just the same she had to wait five minutes by the lavatory and used the time to study a rosette of artificial flowers pinned in her hair. She looked at it from several angles then burst out of the room running downstairs pointing anxiously at where it stuck up at the back. Louise took a pin from her own hair and jammed it in. The soreness gave a sense of security.

She went to the church with another bridesmaid, one of Rose's cousins. Molly was rigid with a sense of occasion but vaguely aware that the bridesmaid next to her was fidgetting and smiling out of the window. In church she was so frightened at standing out and so impressed by the place she didn't realise when the ceremony was over. When they moved to the vestry she thought it was still to come.

Afterwards normality was wonderful. Rose and Michael changed back into the people she knew. Her father looked happy chatting to Mike and her mother flushed and secretive - a combination she recognised as special to public occasions. Her grandmother, no different at or after the ceremony, let Kim out from the kitchen accidentally and he made up for it. More than anyone he knew how to celebrate. His tail wagged hard and slow at first - full of suppressed energy that went to his bottom swinging it in an arc, then cringing with joy he insinuated his body towards one after another. No-one noticed but Molly who hugged him, releasing him like a spring to shoot off and pound guests in the belly and sniff skirts. Ruth grabbed him and dragged him scraping across the carpet back to the kitchen.

With Kim gone Molly looked for someone else to identify with. Rose wasn't standing with Michael but sitting on her own with her back to the wall - the chairs had been pushed there to make room. Molly sat next to her and put her hand in Rose's. Rose smiled, squeezing her fingers. To Molly no face had ever equalled this one. Her cheeks were red and eyes shining - her skin, even her arms, looked powdered.

"You're the prettiest person in the room," she said and Rose squeezed her again. Molly was awed sitting next to her, and when Harry brought Rose a tray of port and sherry she watched her take a dark plum-coloured one and sharply demanded one for herself.

"Of course, Madam, yours is the extra large."

She took it, still watching Rose. Rose sipped. Molly sipped, sipped again, then jumped up, spilling it down her dress.

"It's blackcurrant!"

"What did you expect?"

From this point things changed, Rose was leaving with Michael. Molly was being chastised for the mess on her dress and was now growing desperate. Her uncle picked her up for a quick hug and kiss and looking into his handsome eyes she clung to him.

"We'll be back in two weeks, sweetheart - and we'll be living next door, won't that be fun!" She was greatly cheered by both bits of news but hugged him tighter. "I'll bring you something back from Wales."

"Promise?"

"Of course."

During the fortnight they were away Molly felt things were different. It started the moment they left when Ruth made businesslike noises with glasses while guests were still eating and drinking. The guests had changed. Reassuringly familiar strangers turned into relatives she'd seen quite often and didn't much like. Aunt Carol looked yellower than usual in a green dress. Her father and mother were talking to an aunt she remembered visiting in the country whose face brought back to mind a big untidy garden and a boat trip on the river. She sat by them to listen but they were only talking about the eldest son's new job.

For the next few days her parents seemed unsettled and Ruth was a stranger - tense and slightly irritable. Harry came home looking tired - not keen to play. Molly did her best to bounce him into old habits and went behind his chair one evening to read his book over his shoulder. It didn't say anything she was interested in but she spotted the word 'kiss' on the other page and darted to the other side, banging his head and knocking off his glasses which hung sadly from one ear. She went into shrieks of laughter but he was angry:

"For God's sake sit down and read a book of your own - you don't read enough."

She hung around waiting for the old spark, and feeling lonely went to Louise who looked plump and comforting with her apron still on. Her eyes filled with tears.

"You never cuddle me nowadays," she said accusingly.

Louise's eyes opened in shock, then tenderness. "Don't I, darling?" She sat in the biggest armchair holding out her arms.

Molly leapt on to her lap and tucked her feet up. Tall for her age she had to coil to rest her head on her mother's breast. Warm and relaxed her eyelids started to close but Louise's arm stiffened and she opened them to see her mother looking tensely at Harry who dropped his head as soon as Molly turned to him. She tried to get back again but Louise wouldn't have it:

"You're not a baby - if you're tired go to bed." Sliding Molly off as she stood up and glaring at Harry she took her upstairs.

Molly couldn't sleep. She imagined hands round the edge of the curtain and gas leaking from the tap in her bedroom. An hour later she was still awake listening to Louise restlessly wandering between kitchen and sittingroom.

Harry's glare at Louise when Molly accused her of not

cuddling her had enraged her so much it made her part with Molly, which enraged her further. She couldn't believe he'd the gall to reproach her - Molly barely got time with him now he had his fun elsewhere - he'd had Molly's affections on the cheap and irresponsibly.

She was silently furious after she'd put her to bed. The *Radio Times* was on the table with 'Monkeys, Apes and Men' underlined - and "Which do you feel closest to?" slipped out of her almost clenched teeth.

He left for next door without answering and Louise started crying as soon as he'd gone.

She never challenged him - never said what she thought. He was in the wrong but the temper she couldn't control made it look as if she were. She couldn't move from the circle of fears she'd drawn round herself and not trying to was killing her. She recalled Michael's wedding and the church. Her keen sense of the touching beauty of marriage was called up in contrast to the reality of her own. Ceremonies comforted her, she still believed in absolutes and liked Christmas for that reason but for Harry it was a chance for shopkeepers to get their hands in your pockets. He savaged her needs assuming his were more intelligent. The romance he destroyed as if it were his moral duty gave her an inkling of the harmony she needed. He knew nothing about morality or the facts he was proud of facing. He was a bigger romantic than she could ever be. Her knowledge of life made absolutes necessary if not as aims then as comforts - what else was there?

8

By the time Molly was thirteen she'd given up worrying that it was difficult to satisfy her parents as a pair and enjoyed their company separately.

She was at an all-girls grammar school that exasperated her. Harry'd been overjoyed at her getting there but she'd cried on and off for a weekend. Louise had been inclined to support her desperate aversion to travelling so far to a "snob" school but her involvement only toughened Harry's resolve. Molly miserably identified with the group he described as "vapid and idle-minded who disliked what they didn't understand," and became less clamorous though she went on complaining to her mother when her father was out. It wasn't much relief. Louise seemed angry with her for having got there in the first place. When they'd first heard, Louise had turned from the sink and stared in irritable disbelief. It marked the beginning of her dissociation from the whole business.

Molly would have been depressed at going to any new school, feeling now as settled as she ever could be in the Juniors. She especially didn't want to move to a place that had so many unfavourable, sneering reports. Panic quickly strangled pride and she put everything into trying to talk Harry into getting the sentence converted to life at the local co-ed.

After a year or so at the girls school fear disappeared and misery took over - she was bored and couldn't relate to the others. She couldn't concentrate because there didn't seem to be much to concentrate on. Teachers seemed mostly concerned with the class's behaviour and exams and she wasn't interested in either. She felt cheated most in music where there was no burning interest and no-one felt the lack. Bits of information, bits of listening, bits of theory made her long for weekends and cycle rides with her father, cinema with her mother and long piano practices. She brightened on Friday and by Saturday morning was ready to take on the world.

Sometimes they cycled into the country taking sandwiches - freewheeling down hills, gulping air - stomach in knots of delight - this was life and the rest was dead matter. Long talks when they pushed their bikes uphill or chose to walk to look around were just as important. With Harry she could let go. If she saw something in her surroundings that stirred her up or remembered something from the previous week she could explore it with him. He was totally responsive. She put up with being called intolerant or arrogant for the sake of an open discussion. He loved her hunger for life - disapproving only of some of the routes it took.

At the end of the day they sometimes fell into a happy mesmerised state they didn't want to end, pointing out the obvious for the pleasure of knowing they shared it. If they were too exhausted even for this Harry might keep things going by scaring her. He'd loved making her jump when she was small - her excessive reactions made him laugh. Now he liked shaking her confidence and optimism - adjusting her to reality, he told himself. This way he brought thoughts and panics to light he never expressed elsewhere - she was his intimate, the one he identified with. He'd trot out cynical misgivings, hoping she'd ride them to death with optimism - and putting herself in overdrive she did. Sometimes only quintessential fear would do. He'd tell her an Edgar Allan Poe story remembered in lucid detail and mimed as he spoke - sometimes it worked like an injection. One evening when the bats were flying he broke into a favourite Coleridge quotation - "And having once turned round, walked on and turned no more his head, because he knew a *frightful fiend* did close behind him tread" - and his melodramatic rendering brought her hairs up and turned her pale.

Molly reacted strongly to fear but never took his comments on life seriously. She knew better. His worries about aggression, insensitivity and misunderstanding were meaningless coming from a face full of life and love. They built together an emotional gymnasium they enjoyed differently, returning to it again and again, as they had to games when she was younger.

When he worked on Saturdays Molly went to the local market with Louise and enjoyed herself as much. Intense excitement at the crowds made her walk round with a permanent grin. She hung round favourite stalls where the salesman shouted louder or was younger and fresher-looking. She liked the witty ones best - they shared the fun of it. "Temps" were the unknown. Once a yellow-faced misery of a man held up a bottle of yellow-brown liquid asking if her urine looked like that in the morning and if so to buy his vitamin pills.

Her mother shopped and came back sometimes to ask her opinion on something she'd bought but Molly seldom had one.

There was a live eel stall outside an open-doored cafe full of hot-faced eaters. The eels wriggled over each other between blocks of ice - brilliant and active till blood-covered hands snatched one up and lopped its head off. The rosy face shouting greetings to regular customers made it impossible for Molly to put the two things together. She left them separate but couldn't be persuaded to go into the cafe.

At the far end of the market they finished up in their

regular cafe where there were tremendous opportunities for looking round. Eating a bun and drinking coffee she picked out an interesting couple or family or an energetic, exploratory child or an unusual face - and was gone. Her mother occasionally nudged her into conversation but not for long. Louise liked to share the details of her world but seldom managed it. The only time she was sure of a strong response was when she asked what film to see that evening. Molly had favourite heroes but was basically omnivorous, any love story or adventure would do.

One Saturday she came in from the market, dumped her bags on the table, pulled things out, sniffing and examining in an easy, excited mood, instinctively helping put things away - waiting for seven o'clock and her favourite star playing the lead in a thriller. Louise turned on the radio. Molly loved pop almost as much as "her own" music and couldn't stand still when it was on loud. Hips and arms went wild - energy converted to fantasy about Malden Kane's kisses and back again to the dance then twice as wild.

When Harry came in he got his kiss but no communication. Lunch was served with Molly helping in a vague, abstracted way. Except for her noisy eating the silence continued. She never noticed how her parents ate, obsessed as she was with dreams and a passion for food. Later in her teens she noticed too much and it made mealtimes a torment. For now she was safe in her own world and growing fat.

Harry had worked several Saturdays in succession and missed Molly's chattiness - but it seemed Louise was reaching her, nudging her into doing what she wanted. Even Sunday conversations were shrinking. They used to go on through the meal and into the afternoon - the two of them deaf to Louise's protests at getting "no bloody help."

Now he watched Molly's plump face hung over apples and custard, mouth open, face flushed, eyes bright and vacant, and felt a creeping revulsion from his own.

"The custard's thick, Louise, and too sweet."

She didn't answer, snapping at her spoon. He pushed his dish away - the spoon clacked down on it. No-one noticed. Standing and stretching himself behind Molly's chair he took a deep breath. Molly felt he was taking up too much space, grew tense and couldn't finish her custard.

"Been to the market this morning?"

"Yes." She wanted to get it over and done with.

"Finished your homework?"

"Haven't started."

"Done some practice?"

She didn't answer.

"Done some practice?"

"No."

"Why waste time down the market when you've all that to do?"

"Leave the girl alone." Louise was collecting plates on to the tray. "She's got to have time to relax and be normal."

"What's abnormal about doing homework?"

"You know what I mean."

"You don't know yourself!"

Molly was getting anxious.

"She's a child - she's got to go out. Can't hang around gassing all the time. Funny how homework doesn't come up then!"

Molly got up and banged into the table knocking her custard spoon on the floor. She picked it up, knelt to clean up with a tissue and spat over the bits stuck to the carpet, rubbing hard. Harry poked her in the shoulder with his knee. She looked up to see disgust in his face and stayed on the floor to compose herself but when she got up she was angry.

"The market's fun," she said, "it's full of life."

"So's everything else - especially music. What are your real reasons?"

She looked blank.

"Make me understand why shopping's more exciting than anything else."

She didn't answer.

"Do you still want to be a pianist?"

"You know I do."

"You'll have to do more than want."

Urges to explain and reassure him fell before anger and keeping herself to herself.

"I'm waiting."

Silence.

He turned away with a tight mouth.

She hated what was happening and said, "I like watching people."

"Watching?" he repeated with affected amazement. "Watching bullying fat-arsed women?"

Neither female spoke.

"There was pop music blazing away when I came in - I suppose that's more important too?"

"Yes!"

"It hangs together" - he glanced at her bottom and the custard on her blouse.

Molly blushed so hard she nearly cried. Appeased he put his hands on her shoulders but she snatched herself away and went to the front room, flopping into one of the large chairs and trying to recapture the memory of Malden Kane's screen kisses. One of them in particular had sent her into a burning rapturous state every time she thought of it, but it wouldn't come. She felt empty and looked at the closed piano, picturing herself opening the lid and trying a mazurka. Next minute she was doing it. She repeated the passage that gave her most joy again and again.

Louise in the other room got out her bits of cotton wool and jammed them in her ears. Harry went on with his reading - she was playing at least. Molly's playing was good. If bits were difficult her obstinate repetitions eventually paid off in a technical ease that freed her enjoyment. Her understanding and participation pleased Harry more than accuracy. He had high hopes for her.

After an hour she gave up and knelt in the armchair looking over the back out of the window. She watched the girl opposite, about her own age, go out fashionably dressed. She couldn't find things to suit herself - partly because she was a bit fat but mainly because of the heaviness and pallor of her face. Just the same she was convinced one day she'd find the dress or trousers and top that would blaze her beauty to the world. She sat back on her heels wondering how things were in the other room, then got up, opened her door quietly and sneaked down the passage to listen.

Louise was laughing. The door was open just enough for Molly to look through the crack - Harry had his arm round Louise and she was raising her hand to pull something out of her ear.

That was all right then. She went in.

That evening Molly enjoyed Malden Kane more than ever. It was as well - it had to last her through chemistry and maths homework the following day. Erotic memories seldom survived the onslaught of homework, the sadistic brutality of that could only be relieved in longings to play the piano. The last piece she'd played would come back again and again like the breath of life. In music experience fell into place - richness, vigour, subtlety came back, disproportions were rectified, overall patterns established. She promised herself some playing between each subject.

Sunday was often a day of intense and nervous activity. It was her father's favourite day, the one in which he was sure of her, and Molly too couldn't do without it.

In her classroom on Monday with its radiator-dry air smelling of dirt, ink, books and sweat in familiar proportions her bowels squirmed and a blank gaze came into her eyes. She kept visually in touch with her classmates, smiled, laughed at jokes but had no special friends and still sat on her own. The first five minutes of each day she hid behind the desk lid rearranging books and giving in homework as the monitors came by. A low buzz of conversation stopped when the teacher came in. Middle-aged, fat, formal, insulated in dress and expression she got on with her business. In a moment she called the register. Molly drifted into a state of halfconsciousness but was careful now not to be caught napping. Energy in reserve, she half heard the content of most lessons. Sometimes it broke through completely, she listened and on those occasions enjoyed getting good marks, but hiding out was the prime objective.

Lunchtime was a relief, she ate heartily without liking the food, it seemed to give ballast. If it was too revolting she drank glasses of water to free her from hunger pangs sufficiently to be more selective. She heard a senior girl opposite comment:

"That's why she's fat, you know. It makes you fat, drinking while you're eating. I always wait till the end - then I only have a sip." She looked sure of her facts. The other girl, plump but just as smug, nodded and looked pitying.

Molly was shamed and very angry. She filled her glass so

full the water spilled over, running towards the first girl's plate. She drank noisily, unnerving the plump girl who looked round to see who was watching. A look of angry amazement came on the senior girl's face and it frightened Molly enough to make her crosser still. Molly's ferocious glare made the other feel her dignity was in greater danger from a lunatic than a floating dish and she mopped up with tissues from her blazer pocket.

But Molly hadn't entirely escaped punishment, which turned up in a different form and unexpectedly. Each class had a spy system run by monitors supposedly elected on the basis of popularity. Most girls had been afraid of them before election - they'd been the ones who instinctively put pressure on others, manipulating them through schoolgirl codes, and theirs were the names that sprang to mind when voting. They could be nice but doled it out - were "good types" within a system and in addition their fears and frustrations gave them a fanaticism that could temporarily convert the half-hearted. Among other things their job was to report misdemeanours for discussion in council at the end of each week.

When Molly's name was read out her shame and confusion made her forget the usual procedure.

"Stand, please!" The class teacher supervised from the back - the monitor was in the teacher's chair.

Molly stood, raising the lid of her desk with her thighs. It snapped back suddenly.

"You were seen putting your milk bottle over the playground wall."

Molly said nothing.

"Do you deny it?"

They looked up daring her to. Some victims regularly did and were put through the misery of listening to a chorus of

"Ooh - you dids" followed by a silencing from the chair and a formal request for witnesses - of whom there were always several. Molly didn't move or speak.

"Do you deny it?" The eyes were now just wondering what she'd say.

"No."

"We have agreed to fifteen demerits."

Molly sat down heavily. Thirty demerits in any one week meant detention which was held for an hour or two on Friday evenings. Molly had never had one.

When she got home that evening her shame and sense of exposure was so strong she couldn't eat. She wouldn't talk about it to her parents but went over and over the experience in her mind. Her bowels had grown weak over the last year and by the middle of the evening she'd developed pains which in a now familiar pattern intensified till wave after wave of diarrhoea burst and burned its way out of her. Sudden attacks of this sort were becoming more frequent and Louise worried over them.

When Molly was in bed Louise asked Harry yet again if he thought she'd be better off at the local co-ed. Harry resisted as he usually did but was weakening. He too was worried though he still liked the general effect of the school - he thought it partly responsible for the tensing, or bracing as he chose to call it, which he believed essential to achievement.

9

On this occasion Molly's bowels mended slowly and a fortnight later she was still ill. A doctor said it wasn't an infection and she'd get over it. For her parents the most disturbing side-effect was her lethargy. Each day when she came home they expected her to be herself and had half forgotten anything was wrong and each day they felt the same shock of disappointment and anxiety.

Louise was brooding about it one morning while doing her housework and it slowed her down. Instead of giving the hallway its flick of the duster she abstractedly did the stair rails and hall stand - tidying away the macks and old newspapers trapped under them. She dumped the papers in the bin and saw something drop out - a letter Harry must have forgotten. She took it out of the envelope to see if it was worth saving but got no further than: 'My own darling....'

Checking the address to see if she'd stumbled on someone else's she found her body ahead of her. With a peculiar tingling and blasting of the fingers she'd straightened her arm to distance and focus, pressing her back against the wall. Reading was becoming impossible. Words spilled and splashed into non-consecutive relevance: 'longing.... groin' - no, it couldn't be that - she stared harder and it became 'pain.' She understood through a sequence of shocks slow to disperse and overlapping each other. A couple of sentences towards the end came clear: 'As I lie in bed at night thinking of you my tummy turns over and I wake with a dull ache in the pit of my stomach.'

Louise slid down the wall and sat on the floor, legs stuck out in front and her hands with the letter lying in her lap. Their life together, Harry's and hers, had developed a pattern of contact and friction she'd grown so used to this revelation was as destructive as if she'd known nothing about it. It had seemed he'd been more focussed on home recently - on her as well as Molly. Her mind had fixed on the thought he'd never leave, but her body's reaction now was that he had. The physical pain seemed to be caused by the physical object still in her lap and she shook it off without touching it, pushing herself up from the floor. When it was lying near her foot she ground her heel in it till her calf ached. She couldn't be satisfied and suddenly stood back thinking she mustn't destroy it - Harry must know she'd seen it for its power to be turned against him.

She went past it to the sittingroom and sat down, hands on her belly as if quieting an animal. The strident longings she'd felt when first married were coming back, vicious and frightening. It had been so long since she'd felt anything and years since she'd gripped his buttocks, excited and impatient, waiting for him to make something happen. Angry, confused, it had seemed to her he couldn't be bothered. His mechanical excitement and concentration produced a fury that was vivid and precise and had to be endured and dissipated by silent crying from the eyes. Both she and Harry hated her arousal and between them killed it. She'd pretended she wasn't interested and over the last few years pretence hadn't been necessary.

"Swine, filthy hateful swine!" broke out of her and she was bathed in sweat. So it was alright for that cow. Hilda could express her longing - write it, speak it, look it, act it with God knows what depravity, and Harry went back for more. He held back from her to give to Hilda. She blacked out momentarily and came to, feeling sick. When she came back from the bathroom her mind too had emptied. She sat in her chair waiting for her teeth to stop chattering.

After quarter of an hour she felt well enough to make coffee and went back to the hall to pick up the letter. She folded it, put it in the envelope and put the envelope in her handbag on the table. Her skirt had ridden up when she

56

bent and as she pulled it straight she remembered "fat-arsed women" - then something he'd said to Molly, "There's nothing more disgusting than an oversexed woman" - they'd been watching a barmaid in a television play and Molly'd been grinning, eyes wide.

Trembling violently Louise held her anger down, her mind running through the outrages that made it worse. She'd been what he wanted. She'd reasoned like her mother before her that gratification was only necessary for men. To some extent that had taken care of the "affair" in her mind - Hilda had lowered herself to the level of a man, losing her femininity in masculine lust. But she'd been wrong. Hilda was a victor of many years standing quenching her thirst at Louise's stream - she'd had it all - the only thing she didn't have was Molly.

The contents of the letter worked on her like a poison for the rest of the afternoon but as slowly the effects died down she made a plan she knew she could carry out. When Molly came home she was composed enough to greet her normally and relieved to see she was as usual pale and withdrawn.

It was the same when Harry arrived. He noticed her eyes were darker and fiercer but it added piquancy to her face. He grabbed her arm and kissed her cheek before going into the sittingroom. At supper neither of them noticed she wasn't eating. Molly hardly responded to Harry's questions:

"How'd you get on today?"

"All right."

"Do anything interesting?"

Silence.

"Anything you liked?"

"The Science mistress was away."

"And?"

"We didn't do Science."

He stopped trying and Molly went to her room stopping just long enough to make another plea for a radio of her own.

"So you can listen to pop?"

She slammed the door.

When she'd gone he stretched out in his chair relieved to be rid of the pale-faced burden and started looking at Louise with interest. She still looked different.

"What have you been doing today?"

She asked if he wanted more tea.

Disappointed he nodded, taking his book off the table. By the time she came back he was well into it and she drew the coffee table close to him putting the cup down

He raised his hand without looking and as he turned found it poised over an envelope in the saucer. The writing turned him pale. She was half turned away, her lips moving, but he couldn't hear what she was muttering.

"What?" His throat was so tight it was a whisper.

She faced him, her eyes blazing. "I said, you filthy rotten bastard!"

Uncontrollably frightened - a stupid child-like fear prompting him to get up and put a chair between them - he struggled to make it look like something else but spoke suddenly and too soon and she couldn't understand him. He stiffened in desperation and picked up the letter.

"This, you mean this?" and now the sound was shrill and vindictive. Trying again he said softly, "Louise."

Her face was full of repressed fury and pain. He watched for the right moment. Her eyes were changing by the second - accusation, contempt, disgust, and with intense relief he saw she couldn't say a thing. He became clear-headed. Cautious, very careful not to touch her or say more than was necessary he threw the letter on the table. "It's over - it's finished." He glanced to see how she took it. There was no appreciable difference. "It's all over - Hilda knows it. Why else would she write like that - why risk sending a letter?"

Her face, lined and white, seemed to be responding - her eyes searched the table as for a piece of puzzle.

"I've felt bad about it - so long!" There was a note of insincerity that drew her eyes. "I knew what I was doing - it wasn't helpless love or anything like that." He felt it sounded better that way, less hurtful, but a confused hatred emerged in her face that he leapt to suppress: "Perhaps it was a way of asserting my freedom - an adventure, something new. I've never stopped regretting it."

Louise opened her jaw with difficulty and moistened her lips. "I intend to tell Molly what's hanging over her," she said.

"You wouldn't do that!"

"Wouldn't I?"

He turned away and said in a low voice, "I thought you loved her."

"More than you ever could!"

There were no more moves. Principles as Harry saw them were intrinsic to his understanding of life and he stood naked with the shreds of them flapping in front of a flesh-eater. Instinctive appeasement made him go to the table, take the letter and throw it in the fire.

Louise received the gesture. She picked up the cup and was about to leave when he shouted, "You'll never have cause to hurt her, I swear it!"

The silent tension between her parents exhausted Molly. It lasted for weeks. When Louise was no longer ferocious with rage she was stiff with it. She took her book upstairs hours before bedtime, feigning sleep when Harry came up and aching in the morning from a need to keep separate and not touch him. She slept head under sheet, hands bent from the wrist like paws and the wrists pressed into her face under the cheekbones.

Harry came home from work so wrecked he didn't care what the conditions were - flopping in his chair, reading the paper and dozing.

When the anger level dropped to resentment Louise began to talk a little - briskly, factually to the point, cocky. She developed a hip-barging walk about the house. Doors banged. She gave him food like an irritable waitress. It was an improvement.

Soon when he got back he was greeted by blaring pop music. Louise was in the kitchen waggling her bottom and singing to it. The only time he dared turn it off brought back the frigidity that left him tireder than ever. During this period he left the table every night white with indigestion and Molly had become so remote, so dull and stupid-looking he wondered if he'd dreamed up the old one.

10

One night Molly's trouble was bad enough to call a doctor. He suspected appendicitis and she was whipped off to hospital protesting all the way. Over the next fortnight she was examined by a succession of doctors and students to no-one's satisfaction, but her miserable stay provided an unexpected bonus - she was so happy to be home she came back keener and more alive than her parents had seen her in months.

Harry had completed arrangements for her transfer to the local co-ed while she was away - she was too often ill and was moving too far away from them, the change might bring her back, he thought. He told her the news as soon as she got home and she was overjoyed.

For the first few weeks at the new school Molly could hardly believe her luck. The classrooms were light and airy and hers was on the first floor keeping its outer windows open this warm September. There were trees outside and the room was full of the smell of grass cuttings - even the odd sparrow sat undisturbed on the window frame. The noise in the classroom, greater than at the other school, excited her - so did the boys who were the main source of it - they did things girls never dared to and the girls egged them on. Moral pressures had slackened. When a boy persistently talked, guffawed or got some secret subversion going in a corner at the back Molly saw the French master stride down the gangway, land an echoing clout and go on as if nothing had happened. The rush for the exit at the end of a lesson was full of life. No-one minded her. If she chose to sit on her own she could - they were about their own business.

In a while she started to pay attention to the lessons. They were further ahead in French, Science and Maths. Even the other subjects were handled in a more exciting way. Her illness had cleared by Christmas and Molly was picking up the new work quickly. She received an honourable mention in prayers one morning and spent the rest of the day bubbling with excitement. Harry, delighted at the change in her, nevertheless treated the news as a reminder of the need to "keep it up" - "one couldn't rest on one's oars," she "hadn't begun yet to show them" what she could do. Molly even believed it.

That evening Harry lounged back in his chair with Molly in the comfortable chair opposite - the one that was Louise's. Over the next few weeks, during the evenings at any rate, Molly would make it hers by getting there first. It was her place for turning towards the fire and sprawling her legs and starting a detailed report of the day's doings. Louise sat at the table, elbows on it, listening.

When Molly got tired of that there was a new world next door. Rose had grown stouter since the birth of her two sons and in Molly's view it improved her further. One teatime she was buttering bread, sleeves rolled up. Molly took a loving look at the shiny face that accepted her any time of the day as if her sudden presence were the most natural thing in the world and kissed her hair before squeezing past her in the narrow kitchen.

"Fatties, aren't we?" - she couldn't have said it anywhere else - least of all in her own house.

Rose's jolly "Big bums run in the family!" filled her with a sumptuous pleasure in the characteristic her father despised. She belonged.

She loved the scene when she got to the sittingroom.

Even the approach was different. The house was identical but with everything the other way round. Coming from the kitchen she turned to the left instead of the right and opened the door with her left hand. By the time she got in there was a new reality, her own house had vanished.

Mike was on the far side of the table - pulled out from the wall to make room for the boys - the back of his chair touching the television in the corner. "Hello, Moll! Have some tea!" Always pleased to see her, he tried to get up.

"I've just had some."

"Have a cuppa then?"

Nodding she settled by the fire while he squeezed himself out. She watched, eyes shining. "I've got some news!"

"Come on then, out with it!"

She was sitting on one leg on her chair and dreamily took the tea he'd poured. "I had my name read out in prayers -" she was blushing at the importance of the news and her immodesty in telling it - "I got six 'A's."

"Wow!"- it was what she'd been waiting for. His face had goosepits of excitement if roused. "You're incredible!" he said, his eyes shining in a pocked face.

It was so genuine she went crimson. She didn't want that much. Putting her squashed foot down she sipped tea to stop herself saying it was nothing really - but a bit of honesty would creep out: "Lots of people get marks like that."

Mike squeezed her chin and kissed her forehead.

The two boys were eating. Robert, six, coming to the end of his bread lifted his fair head and freckled face: "Mum!"

The shout was imperative and brought Rose in. "Here it is - give us a chance!"

He took a piece and pasted it thick with jam, messing the jar. When he put it down it messed the tablecloth. No-one minded. Molly, totally happy as she always was in this easy-going house, couldn't help being a little tense about the jam and tenser still about his spitladen chewing. The jam had reached his nose.

Rose brought in a flannel for the two-year-old and cleaned up Robert as well. She put the pot outside Rob's reach and it came within Jim's so she put it on the top of the television behind Mike.

There was silence till the stairs creaked. Molly had a mental picture of her grandmother coming down clasping the handrail, leaning with a possessiveness that looked like gratification. There was an occasional pause. Molly assumed she was lost in thought since she was active and faster on the flat than Rose. She couldn't think of her as old at seventy-two. She was not only full of life but mentally more on the ball than was comfortable. A fast footfall in the passage led to a brisk jerk of the sittingroom door.

"Started without me, I see!"

"Rose did call, Mum." Michael got up helping his mother to her seat. Hers was closest to the fire, Rose's nearest the door.

"Aren't you eating, lass?" Ruth asked Molly over her shoulder.

"I've had mine, Nan."

Rose's manner was strained as she offered her mother-in-law the plate of pilchards in tomato sauce. On the way Robert lifted one of the tails, dragging it half off the plate. Two large plops of tomato sauce went on the cloth. Rose banged down the plate, grabbed his hand and slapped it several times.

He waited till it was over then bellowed. Between bellows he shouted, "I want one!"

Rose slapped him again.

"For goodness sake, leave the boy alone! Can't we have tea in peace for once?" Ruth took the fish she wanted and pushed the plate towards Michael.

"You're the one who makes the fuss," Rose said - "like eating with pigs, you said yesterday." She was redfaced with anger at herself for losing her calm and at Ruth for making her. By slapping Rob she felt she'd been punishing the old woman as well as trying to keep the peace.

Ruth was moved but not to guilt. "No good trying to educate him in one go" - picking the tail fin off her fish with her fork - "general example's best. Fat chance of that with the jam on the telly."

Rose stared at Michael in disbelief. He waved his hand implying "Take no notice."

As the tension eased Robert started up again - wailing for his fish and miserable at getting no comfort after a slapping. When nobody took notice he really gave vent and Jim joined in. The small room held every note, every shriek and gasp, and made the air vibrate. Molly stood to go but couldn't get to the door before Rose, who, scraping back her chair, burst into tears. Molly threw her arms round her and followed her to the kitchen. Rose, gently shrugging her off, went upstairs.

Full of unsatisfied compassion Molly went back to her own house and made a tearful report.

"Not again!" Harry said, and there was something in his tone that made Molly sorry she'd mentioned it. He got up and she spotted the steely look that gave rise to so much tension and so much family respect. He set himself up as judge and they took him at his own evaluation. Louise followed him to the back door.

"Leave 'em alone," she said, "don't interfere, it's none of your business."

He walked out without looking at her and half an hour later Louise went too. Molly went to the front room to practise. Whatever was going on next door went on through two and a half hours of it.

Next morning, expecting things to be normal, she found both parents quiet and remote and in the evening Louise mentioned in a toneless voice that she'd better get her rubbish out of the box room as Ruth was going to live with them. Molly's first reaction of delight met no support. She thought there must be something wrong she hadn't understood:

"Is she going to stay for good?"

"Yes." Harry was answering from behind his paper but she could tell what he felt.

"Is Grandma to sleep in the box room?"

"Where else?" Louise said irritably - "want her to sleep with you?"

It was a silly question. Even so Molly wouldn't have minded. Ruth could be fun and someone to talk to when she wasn't moody.

By the end of the week Ruth's things had been installed and she'd slept her first night with them and over the weekend there was a great deal of talk about property. Molly gathered her grandmother had been robbed by Rose, that having signed over the house - "at a fair price," Harry reminded her - she found herself cheated out of the kitchen, out of comfort, out of respect. Molly's eyes filled with tears, knowing it couldn't possibly be Rose's fault or Michael's. Ruth was mixed up. On the other hand she was so distressed something real must have happened. Depressed, Molly went about her business and spent the weekend reading, since the piano had been forbidden by all parties.

Their lives developed a new structure and Molly over the

next year was changed by it. She was no longer quite so close to anyone. Ruth went for a stroll during her practices - she spoke support but couldn't stand their duration or volume. She adopted Louise's habit of cotton wool in the ears and even Harry found himself arguing for quieter occupations when she'd finished her homework. Molly felt less joy in playing but less able to do without it. She'd no friends and the solitary life made her dependant on her family still. Reading was Harry's joy and he pushed his own habit, bringing home books she didn't like. She hated the local library, was oppressed by its quiet and airlessness and most of all confused and impatient with the cataloguing system. She'd spend an hour searching in it or be side-tracked by inviting covers on he shelves. At the end she might have found a thin volume of stiltedly translated tales or indifferent verse - if she read at all it was always poetry and legends. Harry brought home some Rupert Brooke and took pleasure in looking in on her in the front room to find her gazing out of the window with the open book in her lap. Better than dreaming pop and film stars, he thought, but for Molly they belonged to the same bloodstream.

In her bedroom she got the best view of the poplars at the end of the garden and it was there she recited the poems she liked best - but soon lost interest. Pleasure in the trees took over - glistening black trunks, branches moving like animals, a bird cleaning its beak. Finally she'd throw the book on the bed.

On one such occasion she decided to take Kim for a walk. Nowadays she treated him like an object. He'd become old and lazy and stank when he lay in the sun. She stirred him with her toe.

"Come on, lazy pig!"

Kim rolled over and spread his back legs, eyes firmly

shut. The weight of skin round his jaws pulled his mouth back and he looked as if he were smiling. She looked at his pink stomach with patches of brown pigment and colourless warts, and touched with affection and disgust rubbed his belly. He spread his legs wider, still smiling.

"Come on," she said prodding.

Nan was in the chair behind them. "Leave him alone girl - let him rest."

"I'm taking him for a walk."

"He doesn't want to, poor thing."

"It's not what he wants but what's good for him!"

"You remember that when you do your homework!"

Molly looked angry. Smart-Alec, interfering adults, all tarred with the same brush, grinding their own axes. She was delighted at the thought of them grinding, filthy with tar, and yanked the dog to his feet by his collar. She fetched his lead.

After a moment of relief at being out she started staring into cars on the main road for good-looking drivers. She dragged Kim past lampposts he'd marginally sprayed, hauled him from squatting positions in a panic of embarrassment and Kim lumbered dismally behind till her pace slowed down. On her side of the road there was a nursery and garden centre and she stared into its glasshouse over a low brick wall. Kim took his opportunity. She was looking at the plants for a while then watched a reflection in the glass of three soldiers opposite standing outside a Territorial Army centre. She looked at her own reflection and pulled in her stomach, convincing herself her figure looked just well-developed. She paid no attention to the pale fat face moving like a moon.

She started off again at a smarter pace and Kim, yanked into activity and not ready for it, jerked her back, ruining her outline. When she'd passed the soldiers and realised they hadn't noticed she walked back to stare in the glasshouse once more, then set off making a few remarks to the dog that could be heard:

"Come on, Kim, there's a good boy, you're so slow!" - the tone was highpitched and maudlin.

She was noticed, and blushing turned the corner. Even now she couldn't let it rest. In her embarrassment she hadn't been able to see *how* she'd been noticed. Had they liked her? Overcome by the need to know, defying panic and shame, she walked back, head up, tummy in. This time when she looked in the glass one of them had his arm raised in her direction and was saying something. The one with his back to her had lowered his head and his shoulders were jerking. He was laughing. She wound the dog's lead round her hand a couple of times in an anguish of humiliation - bracing herself against his body, keeping him close. They went home.

The following year the Autumn edition of the school magazine came out and Molly was reminded of the brilliance and energy of one of the boys. He was in the class above hers and had just been praised in prayers for eight 'A's in O levels. He was rugger captain, an honour usually reserved for the upper sixth, and it was said he'd be made school captain next year. The headmaster's regular rejoicings in the rugger results and praise of Tom's captaincy might have been enough but he only really came to Molly's attention through the magazine. He'd written an article on hiking in Scotland and a short poem on a storm. The poem was too academic for her but the article was fascinating. She took in everything. He'd gone with friends, sleeping overnight in youth hostels till they ran out of money and when the warden wouldn't take his watch as a guarantee they slept out on ground sheets under bushes at a lakeside. The sleep had been sound till five in the morning when they woke in a heavy mist, cold and hungry. That was all, but it was told with a vivid matter-of-factness that bowled her over. Independence, energy, lack of fear.

In her customary dreamy way she'd accepted his existence without spotting who he was. He was pointed out going into the diningroom and the girl she asked made an issue of it: "*There* he is," she said so he heard. He turned, looked irritated then faintly amused and went in.

An overpowerful engine leapt to life in Molly. She was throbbing with its vibration but had no idea how to engage the clutch. She put herself somewhere quiet to find out what had happened. Within seconds of crossing the playground to a corner of the playing field she knew exactly what she felt. The feeling was so much more violent than a crush on a film star it hadn't seemed to come from the same source, especially as it was accompanied by a mastering sense of her own power.

She hadn't expected him to be handsome. Cramped into a school blazer his shoulders looked wide and powerful. Regular features, strong precise body movement, a quick, slightly hostile look with inaccessibility inbuilt, fine thick brown hair and above all a beautifully shaped full red mouth - she recalled them so vividly it hurt. The memory kept coming back - she couldn't let it go. Weak, hot, she sat down suddenly on the grass, staring unseeing at the rounders practice in front of her.

Molly found out as much as she could about him, asking indirectly of several girls - even staff - but taking care he was never the subject of conversation. For more personal details she had to be more forthright and hoped to disguise her interest by an offhand or contemptuous manner:

"I suppose being so important he makes the girls take it in turns."

Mavis, a thin quiet girl with a mild manner, could be relied on to answer straight: "He's got a girl - Betty Redford. I don't know who else he's been out with."

"Do you like him?" Molly asked.

"I don't know - he's a bit much - thinks a lot of himself."

"Why shouldn't he?" Molly was cross with herself.

"He's very clever," Mavis said.

Amazed at the girl, Molly came out in her true colours: "Don't you think he's sexy?"

"I don't know, he frightens me a bit."

She looked at her incredulously; perhaps he hadn't got so many girls. She blushed and her eyes brightened.

Molly had a music exam coming up and it seemed easier now to put herself to the work. In spite of Louise's frail nerves and Ruth's anger she managed with her father's help to establish the precedence of practice over everything else. Louise was proud of her playing - the music was another matter, it cut into the world she built, leaving her frayed and anxious, and the urgency in Molly's playing worried her - the girl asked too much from everything - "Like her father," Ruth once said, but it wasn't true.

11

Molly passed but not to her satisfaction. The strain of playing under exam conditions and knowing they were listening to technique more than to what she wanted to communicate made things hopeless before she started. In fact her technique in exams was no good - she was at her worst, playing defensively. Frustration could bring in a crude ruthlessness and obstinacy.

Her family was pleased with the result. She told herself it was only at home communication existed. She knew that at this stage she couldn't express herself through music as she wanted but at home she was satisfied to work towards it, absorbed, obsessive - almost a private achievement. She was beginning to switch off from judgment. It alarmed Harry because for him judgment was the great stimulater. She developed the habit of practising till she felt free from technical anxiety so as to be able to explore the piece properly and was sometimes held back by the very intensity of her need to get there. Every inflexion of delight and communication the music offered had to get expression and if she failed she fell into pits of depression and lethargy.

Sometimes, feeling what she wanted was impossible and always would be, she'd reject the whole business. During one such period her uncle asked if she still wanted to be a famous pianist when she grew up and the description sounded exciting but insulting.

"I want to *live* when I grow up!" was her answer.

"No, I mean your job - do you want to play for a living?" The hurt now went two ways - she'd never play for a living nor live for playing.

"I want to get stuck into life like an animal in raw meat - playing might be part of the result."

Michael saw she had a point and didn't want to upset her.

"Raw what?" Harry said prodding her leg with his foot. "Revolting beast!" He'd been staring at the fire and at the mottle marks on his mother's legs from too much exposure to it. The disgust and contempt in his voice angered Molly.

Louise and Mike were sitting opposite each other at the table. Mike, legs crossed and turned towards the centre of the room, looked up at Molly hoping she'd ignore it. She did.

"At her stage we all are," he said in relief. "Everything we see and feel is for us and our appetite's enormous. I'd like to feel like that again!" He winked at Molly with a slight tuck of his head to one side.

Ruth's ball of wool rolled off her lap and as Harry bent to pick it up his words squeezed out: "It's not the feeling I'm questioning but the expression."

Louise gave a puff of the lips: "How pointless can you get?"

Harry glanced at the grin Molly was giving her. "What you're missing, old girl," he said without looking at her, "is that choice of expression can say more about an individual than the thought. We're none of us original."

Now Molly exploded. She was sick of his smudging of life. "But we're all of us unique - when did you last take a science lesson?" He didn't answer immediately so she went on: "Don't you like sinking your teeth into things?"

"Like a dog, you mean? - you think it's the best way of enjoying the flavour?"

"Sometimes it's quantity that counts. You've lost your appetite - I'll never do that!"

Her cockiness drove him crazy. "Gutsy and crude - we're all like that at your age. Don't imagine you're unique - it's all been thought and felt before."

"Puts you off, does it?"

His taut, injured look made her stomach turn over - she loved him too much, and dropped to her knees putting her head on his lap.

"Just like a woman," he said, pushing her off, "no logic - what's it got to do with being put off?"

She knew she'd reached him and kissed his leg and hugged it.

"Next step in a woman's repertoire," he said - "retreat to emotion!" His eyes shone with angry victory and she sat back on her heels, disbelieving:

"You can't be *that* stupid!"

With melodramatic exaggeration Ruth put her knitting down. "Don't *dare* speak to your father like that!"

Molly looked from one to the other. "My God, what a life!" she said, and stood up.

She was grabbed from behind and Mike forced her to sit on his knee. "What's up, Mollikins? Molly's in a temper, Molly's in a temper!" - bouncing her up and down as if she were small, the physical effort sounding in his voice. She wrenched herself away but saw his startled, hurt expression and flung her arms round him kissing him several times on cheeks and head and mouth.

"That's enough, Molly, for goodness sake!"- Louise grabbed her arm - "calm down."

Molly took off to brood and listen to her new radio.

Louise took less and less part in arguments. She'd developed migraine over the past two years and claimed it was caused by the "eternal argy-bargy." Nevertheless the evening pastime Molly and her father liked best was just that. Molly'd rake over the day's events and some sort of discussion or row would follow. She saw her mother's face drawn in mute tension but couldn't let go the other end of the bone. To Louise everything they thought was pointless or exaggerated. It disturbed her because the more they followed their tongues the further away they got from reality as she saw it - worse still, it made them touchy and alien.

She challenged them one evening. Harry'd been describing the state of feeling at work since the proposal to amalgamate two departments. There'd been several meetings in which they'd aired their anxieties, he said, and in the end he'd got fed up and refused to go. He was a good speaker and they saw it as letting them down.

"So you were," Louise said.

"But we never got anywhere, nothing we said made sense. The central board was making a simple suggestion that didn't affect work or pay, only the pattern of work, so why the fuss?"

"Did you say that?" Louise asked.

"Of course."

"No wonder they got fed up with you!"

"It wasn't that that bothered me but the remark got into the minutes and an official response to it came back at the next meeting: 'The decision will be made on the basis of a consensus of opinion. If no conclusion is reached the central board will make the final decision.' Isn't that what I was saying? For weeks we haven't made up our minds. We understand it'll be more economical and probably more efficient but we fart around so much they'll do it anyway!"

Mike agreed with Harry but said with feeling, "Office clerks' nerves are always frayed - I should know. It's so easy to feel bored and put upon."

Molly joined in with a description of staff faces and tempers after their meetings, amusing both men by miming them.

Louise raised her head from the hand propping it. "How come you dissociate yourselves?" - it was to Harry but included them all.

"I don't," Michael said defensively.

"Harry does, he feels he's better than they are."

Harry was taken by surprise. "I don't! I take them seriously enough to disagree with them" - he looked at Molly for corroboration.

"You *were* dissociating yourself - you all were - I don't understand any of you."

They looked at each other as if this were thoroughly unjust but Louise went on, "Of course they must feel they're taking part - that they count - that their opinions and anxieties matter. No-one can live feeling they don't matter - they might as well die!"

"Don't be so melodramatic - my point isn't that they don't matter but that they're making a fuss over nothing."

"But they don't feel they are. There'll be a change, they'll be working with different people or the work will be different."

"Not even that. The people will be the same, the offices the same. Personally, I could do with a change. Even the work will be the same, though in some areas the way we do it will alter to adjust to the two departments running as one."

"Well, that's it then!" she said - "the way they'll have to do it is worrying them. They don't know if they'll take to it - change makes people anxious."

"Too bad. Things *have* to change."

Molly had her own reactions. She was cross at Harry's air of superiority, respected his view but felt her mother was right, anxiety did matter. He adopted what looked like an impersonal angle, but it wasn't - Louise only appeared defeated because she felt she was. Her angle was so openly personal, Harry's concealed. Molly had a sudden urge to do something about it but the effort of going against him made her tone wrong and she sounded vicious:

"Come off it, Dad, we're all anxious - you're anxious never to lose an argument!" He pulled a mouth but she went on: "That fuss isn't *your* fuss - that's all you're saying. Your pride's hurt, being identified with it."

He was at a loss for a moment and plumped for parental indignation: "You see yourself as one of the cringers and whiners?"

"See what I mean?" she said but blushed, glancing at her mother to see if she were hurt.

Louise's eyes blinked rapidly, looking more tired than anything. After a while she stood up and said, "I'm going to bed - I've another attack coming on. You can get your own bloody supper!" and left the room.

Mike invited them to have it with him next door.

The following morning was Saturday and Louise went shopping without Molly who took the opportunity to do more practice. After an hour of obsessive repetitions of a tricky passage she saw Ruth standing at the open door, hand on the knob:

"I wondered when you'd notice!" She had one slippered foot forward as if to come in and looked ready for something. "Why's a young girl like you stuck indoors hammering when you should be out with a boy? Fifteen now, aren't you? High time you had one!" She left feeling she'd given her something to think about.

It had already dawned on Molly it wasn't really her fatness and pallor that put her out of the running. A girl as fat as herself in her class had a string of boys. She suspected they weren't romantic relationships and decided she didn't want to be 'liked' or be 'a good sort' but to be passionately loved. If she couldn't have that she'd go without. She felt she wasn't ugly - her real trouble was something she couldn't do anything about. Rather than worry about the unchangeable she concentrated on the disadvantages that might go away - fatness, spots and shyness. She started practising smiles and interested talk in front of the mirror to see how she looked. Discounting self-consciousness she could see what was wrong. The practice was very low-key but her face still betrayed her - there was always too much. She was a clown.

At home her intensities were accepted and the balance was good. At school the alternations between dreamy remoteness and passion for music and poetry isolated her as they always had. In debates, in spite of self-consciousness, she'd find herself bursting out with something she couldn't hold in - enough to frighten any boy into cancelling ideas of approaching her. This was especially hard to accept as she'd have responded to the crudest if she thought they meant it. She tried countering false impressions by laughing conspicuously at the antics of the most randy boy in the class. He wasn't good-looking but it didn't matter, she loved his crudity, glowed in its presence and felt released.

Having discovered the ruse worked Ruth tried it again a couple of weeks later:

"Done anything about it yet?"

"What?"

"Getting a boyfriend."

Molly barely paused in her playing. "Don't worry about me, I'll marry a navvy when I grow up."

"Don't talk silly!" She came over to put her hand over Molly's and stop her. "You could get yourself a nice boy if you put yourself on a diet."

"I don't want a nice boy!"

Ruth raised her finger. "Don't talk silly. You're a good-looking girl underneath. Your father was such a handsome man - still is - and you favour him, I'm happy to say." She stood back and appraised her. "Now why don't you put on some make-up? Not much, mind. Do it nicely and go out for a little walk. You could take Kim for company."

"I'm not going for a walk, Nan, I'm going to practise."

"I tell you you're ruining your chances with all this stuff and your pale face. You don't get out enough - not enough fresh air." Molly turned as if to go on playing. "Look, I'll tell you something p'raps I shouldn't -" she was pressing on Molly's arm.

Molly looked at the keen nose and excited grey eyes and waited. Ruth seemed to be changing her mind.

"Don't you want to have boys?"

Angry to be back there again she put her hands on the keys but Ruth went on:

"There's no reason why you shouldn't. Your father could have had any girl he wanted, any girl at all. Such lovely white teeth, and tall - and his eyes always clear and alive."

Molly rolled up her own. "What's it got to do with me, Nan?"

The look of indecision was still on Ruth's face. "Any girl at all, I tell you. Your mother got him by being there - she'd known him so long - she flattered him, hung around shamelessly."

"He must have liked it."

"But he never had a chance to look round, she never let him alone, so he married beneath him - couldn't help himself."

Molly moved to get off the stool but Ruth pressed her bony fingers in her shoulder. Suddenly she remembered hearing Ruth and Louise rowing in the kitchen that morning and after it Louise had gone out without her. Her mother's voice had been loudest - strident and bullying. Molly'd been in bed and couldn't make out what was being said. She'd passed her grandmother on the landing - face flushed, mouth working.

"Your mother - " Ruth was trembling and paused for emphasis - "your mother came out of the gutter - the youngest of thirteen kids of a drunken Irish labourer. He used to get drunk and wallop the lot of 'em - wife included."

"Your father was a labourer, wasn't he?"

Red blotches appeared on Ruth's cheeks. "Your grand-father was a carpenter and a good and gentle man - a craftsman. We were of good family. My family would have been rich if we hadn't been cheated out of a patent by father's second cousin. Toby Sharp made a fortune out of it."

"I've heard that one before!" Molly blew air from her nose. "And if Grandad never hit anyone it makes him better natured not better class."

"Now, madam, just listen to me - I've not finished yet." Ruth rested on the piano a hand arthritis was turning into a fist and searched Molly's face. "Remember Hilda? No, I don't suppose you do. Good-looking blonde woman, going to be a teacher. Your father knew he'd made a mistake and took up with her." She enjoyed delivering the news so much she half expected Molly to join in, and nodded trium-phantly. Molly had gone pale and looked confused. "Well, not that it's right, mind, he's married and all, but what can you expect?"

Molly stood up, found Ruth was still blocking her, pushed past and swore at her.

"That's your mother coming out! Swear at me and I'll tell your father."

"Do!" Molly said, white with rage. "I wish you would and

I'll tell him word for word what you've told me."

Ruth blushed, standing erect. "I should think you'd be ashamed!"

Molly left, incredulous.

For weeks she was remote with Harry but no closer to Louise. He began to wonder if he'd hurt her in some way. She wanted to rage and blame but couldn't. Excitement and interest had gone out of everything.

Then Rose's sister came to live in the neighbourhood and when the family visited for the first time Molly went with Louise to meet them. She'd heard there was a son a couple of years older than herself and had tried to pump her mother before meeting him.

"I've not seen them for twelve years, how should I know what he looks like?" Louise said.

"What was he like as a baby?"

"Like all babies - fatter than most."

Just the same Molly began to speculate. If he were fatter than most he'd have a healthy appetite. The theory extended to sexual appetite.... she put on a dress too small, nipping her in at the waist. Smallish waist, tight bust, skirt discreetly full - she was pleased with the effect and loosened her hair after lightly powdering her face.

She hung back when they approached Rose's best room, listening for his voice. He wasn't speaking. She tried to get a glimpse of him through the crack of the door as it opened.

"Come on in, Molly, don't hang about - come and say hallo." Louise pushed the door wide so Molly had to move but the boy was still hidden. She went in and stood stiffly in front of Rose's sister Mary.

"How you've grown! What a difference since I saw you last!" Mary got up and kissed her. She had a round, inexpressive face and gentle manner. "What about George," she said mildly, "he's even bigger."

Molly blushed and turned to face him. Still a little fat, he had a face built for laughing and thick fair hair that flopped over his forehead as he leant towards her. He raked it back with spread fingers. His next move was more than she'd hoped for. With a spectacular grin of white teeth he put out his hand and touched her arm to suggest she sit next to him. She was overcome by the smile and from that moment deaf and blind to everything but his closeness. Staring into her lap and sometimes sideways at his shoes she felt the sofa move under her when he moved. She could smell his clothes - dry and fibrous tweed jacket with oily undertones and a smell of sweat that drugged her. They were totally preoccupied, each reading the other's almost imperceptible movements - even stillness communicated.

Molly left with Louise half an hour later without having said a word but as she was going they reached an understanding in a glance that was almost too articulate for her.

From then on whenever George and his mother came to visit Rose Molly went next door whether Louise came or not and as their confidence grew they arranged to be alone sometimes. In the Spring George took her round the garden, first to look, then to weed. He tried making her squirm with reports of a disembowelled bird he'd found - guts crawling with maggots - and later gave a graphic description of the texture and colours of the snot his friend had sneezed out at school. She knew she was being tested and squirmed at the first story, but not too much, and laughed and grimaced at the second. She slapped him playfully and called him "filthy pig." She seemed to have passed. Nothing further happened.

George's visits were few because he came under cover of his mother's and these were mostly when he was at school. It was months before he was told she played the piano and then she was terrified the relationship would end. He said he'd like to hear her and she played him a short piece - they were in her own front room for the first time. Afterwards she sat in the deep armchair squashed against the sofa he was sitting on. They rested their arms on the arms of the seats in an active stillness focussed in the supposedly relaxed hands - silently stalking their courage. It took ten minutes to shift so the little fingers touched. The next move followed quickly. His finger stroked Molly's and gave her a sensation so exquisite she began to lose consciousness.

One Thursday evening George came through the garden from Rose's. He'd never visited on a week night before and burst in on the family, tense with special news:

"We're going to America!"

Molly was sitting at the table with her father, doing Geometry. She was so disappointed she couldn't speak.

"Only for a year," he said looking at her - "on business."

Harry jumped up. "How splendid, how exciting!" It was the first time he'd ever shown an interest in George and he looked round at Molly: "Wouldn't it be great if we were!"

In a quiet voice she answered, "Yes."

George was clearly happy but as he watched her there was a tightness in his face that mollified her. "I thought you'd come next door with me and say goodbye - wave me off, sort of."

"Yes."

Harry realised for the first time the youngsters cared for each other.

They left, shutting the kitchen door tight behind them. It was dark. Instead of walking to the back door they hesitated and George put his arms round her and kissed her. The sharpness and beauty of sensation made her tremble and he had to coax her to the back door where he kissed her again. When they were in the garden they could just see each other. George's red soft mouth and roused eyes were a revelation of beauty. She took his hand and put it round her waist where it moved instantly to her breast. They kissed and caressed till panicking at the ferocity she broke away, hurting from the wrench and going dazed into her aunt's house.

In there Rose and his mother were talking excitedly. The youngsters sat in silence pretending to listen. It was late when Harry came in to remind Molly she'd homework to finish. George asked if she could come back afterwards. Harry nodded.

"Come on, Moll, buck your ideas up!" He was pushing open the back door and Molly was going through the same dark kitchen. She didn't hear what he said when he pushed her into her seat.

"Eh?"

He looked hard at her. "Do you?"

"Do I what?"

"Oh, for Christ's sake!" - pushing her arm off the table.

"I didn't hear what you said."

"I asked if you wanted to pass this bloody exam. This is your worst subject and the exam's next week."

"Of course!"

"Well, get down to it!"

But she couldn't make sense of the problem in front of her and couldn't pay attention when Harry explained it. He finished the sums for her and tossed the pencil on the table. Still dazed she was now anxious, tense and guilty. He was angry and it wasn't just over the homework - it was as if he'd finished with her. When he left she sat, hollowed out, on her own in silence.

Later she went back next door. When she kissed George goodbye secretly just before he left, she felt nothing. Waving him off she could hardly believe it - trying again and again to recapture the beauty and excitement of the first kisses.

12

During the next months Louise found everything too much for her. At opposite ends of the age range Ruth and Molly made demands needing opposite extremes of tolerance. Between them they were destroying her.

Ruth's insatiable appetite for food and warmth no longer roused compassion but disgust. At first she was touched but now she watched her come pushing and tottering with excitement - she'd aged since she changed house - twenty minutes too soon for every meal, making it impossible for Louise to be late. She saw her turn her chair to the fire each evening in a way that forced others to sit to the side or behind, and found herself eternally angry. It was the only emotion she seemed to feel nowadays and it made her spiteful. Sometimes she gave the old lady burnt chips buried under good ones or a thick but not meaty end of pie, telling herself hunger wasn't discriminating. She made up for it by giving her large quantities of the most filling foods and this gave Ruth opportunity to comment on the boring or lousy cooking. She was furious when the complaint was made in front of the others. Even over the chair they waged battle. When Ruth was out of the room it was moved back and the other chairs pulled forward but if Louise left she found it back in its old place.

Molly's physical needs didn't upset her. They were just as spontaneously avid and selfish but acceptable and she was pleased to gratify them. It seemed to be all that was left of their relationship and it was Molly who was the more destructive of her peace, especially when in the Spring the girl was obsessed with her O Levels but not able to get down to work. She sat around with a pale face and abstracted expression and when Louise wasn't burdened with silence it was with the noise of the piano. She didn't complain - she was proud of her and sorry for her miserable face. Molly practised a couple of hours after school most days either there or at her teacher's home while he visited wealthier students. She also practised in the morning before leaving for school and over the weekends four or five hours a day. The tutor, an old man and a well-known in his time, often called at their house and on these occasions the level of intensity rose like a flood and Louise waited for lesson and conversation to be over. When she could flush him out she scrambled back to normality but felt fearful and exhausted.

Harry on the other hand was happier than he'd ever been. He loved Molly's obsession but kept goading her about O Levels. He helped her by reading whatever she had to and chatting about it and sometimes it went on late in the evening till she'd lost a little of the rigid obstinacy that seemed to take over at exam times. On occasions their old-style chats took over and after the tutor's visit the talk might be about music and Molly'd be extra excitable. The pitch rather than volume of their voices often woke Louise and she'd appear in the doorway in pyjamas with her hair in curlers. Red-faced with anger, her body tense and bright with it, the contrast between her appearance and quivering strength of feeling made them want to laugh and if it broke out it was hysterical. She'd leave speechless. If she was calmer she'd leave after a short rebuke and Molly might follow.

At this stage Harry felt he understood Molly so well and identified with her so much that if her responses were different from his he was hurt - but it made attempts to identify with others less necessary and rewarding. He seemed almost completely happy and Molly felt she depended on his instant understanding for survival. Beyond it nothing mattered but music.

If Louise tried to make him see what she thought was happening to Molly - that intensity was part cause of her ill-health and that he was encouraging it - she saw only disappointment and condemnation in his face. She was jealous, he thought. Disgusted and impressed, furious and servile, she wore herself out in extremes. She thought she saw Molly losing all robustness, all the natural greedy animal energy she loved most in her, and saw Harry rejoicing in it.

Raging against the three of them as well as herself brought on more attacks of migraine. The headaches and strange frightening lights preceding them sometimes confined her to a dark room for two or three days and it was almost a relief. She was ill and gave up feeling. Sometimes afterwards she felt unexpected joy in being alive. Harry and Molly dreaded the attacks and came closer to her, which nearly made them worth it. It was then she'd try to make contact with them along the old lines:

"If we didn't lead such stressful lives we'd all be better. I wish we could relax. Your tummy's getting worse, Molly, like my head," she said one teatime while Ruth was visiting Michael next door.

"It's O Levels, Mum. I'll be better when they're over."

Louise shook her head, starting to point out it'd been getting worse for years, when Molly burst into tears. She got up and cuddled her daughter's head to her breast. "What is it, my pet? Tell mummy."

Molly cried harder, as she had as an infant when Louise gave unconditional comfort.

Harry sat with his knife in his hand, eyes full of surprise and anxiety. "What's the matter, Moll?"

Molly spluttered and heaved and pieced together her anxiety about the exams and her inability to sleep. "I can't sleep - I never get any good sleep, what can I do? Can I sleep with you, Mum, for a bit - just till after the exam? - I've been wanting to ask you for ages."

Louise kissed her daughter's hair. "Silly girl, why didn't you tell me before?" She was pleased, her face looked relaxed and reassured and she looked over Molly's head at Harry who raised his eyebrows - but he nodded. "You sleep with me for a bit then and see how things work out," she said.

For a few nights after this Molly slept well and her spirits improved. In time, in spite of the exams, she seemed almost her old self and even gave up playing the piano during the few weeks of O Levels. Afterwards she stayed relaxed and was soon ready for jokes, fun and exciting conversations. At this point she began to find her mother's presence at night a strain but was afraid of losing it. When they went to bed at the same time Louise got to sleep first - usually within minutes - while Molly, burying her head under the bed-clothes, raced to get there before her but never made it. Once or twice she went to bed before Louise which felt like a major sacrifice as her mother went so early but she only lay awake missing her talks with her father and when Louise came in she was wider awake than ever. In the light from the street lamps Molly watched the muscles of her face relax, saw her mouth come slightly apart and waited for the faint regular popping noises from her throat. They weren't loud or especially unpleasant, but slowly she built up an unjustifiable rage. She nudged Louise, who turned over, then tried to sleep in the interval, only to be overtaken by irregular, fullblooded snores. She got out of bed, went to the lavatory making as much draught as possible and jumped back in, waking her. She couldn't risk the terrors of going back to her own room but developed a series of harrying tactics that at some time or other paid off in terms of her own rest. Louise always fell asleep again from sheer exhaustion.

One breakfast time Louise surprised them all by telling them she'd taken a job as assistant stores clerk in a local factory. Molly'd been up only five minutes and was in the trance-like state preceding panic to get out on time. She stared at her mother then at Harry.

"It's been fixed for a week. I start this morning!" Louise had a smile of pleasure that was disarming and confusing.

"Come off it!" Molly said and looked at her father. He was as surprised as she was.

"It's a surprise," Louise said. "I need to get out. I don't want any discussion over it - it's only a morning job. I get home at two o'clock every day. In the summer holiday you can do the housework for me, Moll!" She grinned at her.

The household accepted Louise's decision almost as simply as she'd made it and Harry seemed extra pleased and affectionate towards her.

Louise greatly enjoyed her new life working as assistant to a woman ten years older than herself who carried an ample body with dignity and let it be known she'd be happy to carry it to the altar a third time. She had an inner assurance and sense of achievement Louise envied and they became close friends. Louise's crude sharp humour amused and opened up Mrs Barton to the point where the two women could exchange confidences. The relief of talking to another woman and disinterested party about rows at home and of being venomous or extravagant when she felt like it was miraculous for Louise and left Mrs Barton in no doubt as to her underlying commitment, while Mrs Barton was stimulated by affections and grievances sharper than her own. Louise began to look healthier and younger, regaining some of her old good looks. With a little of the extra money she bought new clothes - the design and colour reflecting her brighter outlook. She had her hair cut and restyled - which was a blow too strong for Molly who burst into tears when she saw it. She couldn't bear to see her mother a stranger. The reaction daunted Louise for a time but Harry liked it and she kept the new things going.

Sometimes Louise came home with interesting tales to tell - reports of cheeky conversations between herself and the men who came for supplies. Her eyes sparkling, cocky but dismissive, she told Molly one of them had pinched her bottom. Molly was very pleased and when she saw Harry afterwards felt a delightful sense of power as if she and her mother had had their own back.

About this time there was a school concert. Molly had occasionally played hymns in prayers but had never agreed to anything else. Harry'd been cross with her for it, accused her of false modesty and asked how she ever hoped to be a concert pianist. Molly was obstinate without explanation.

In fact she felt it would make things more difficult at school. She'd made some friends, enjoyed company and jokes and recently not felt beyond the pale as far as boys were concerned. One boy in her class had written a mock ballad called 'Sir Hugh and Lady Molly' which he read out in an English lesson and the girl behind her poked her in the back. The ballad described the feats of daring Sir Hugh was forced to accomplish before he could win the Lady's hand. Molly turned to look at Hugh Barlow, a fresh-complexioned thin-faced boy sitting four rows behind and he was blushing and grinning.

Suddenly she remembered his fooling about - "Ssst, Molly - watch this!" - he'd pinged a bit of inky blotter on another boy's neck. The boy jumped, turned, grabbed and been fought back - Hugh's eyes flicking to Molly to see she was watching. A number of similar incidents came back and she leaned back in her seat, confused, blushing and happy.

When the school concert came this year she had more confidence - when she was asked to play she agreed. More than anything she wanted to get Tom Parsons' attention. She wasn't afraid. She'd watched his concentration and enjoyment in the music club - a face that tried to betray nothing but betrayed everything - energy, intensity, a joy that was in the very bend of his neck while he kept himself to himself studying his feet. She studied him - sensuality in every line of the face, but cool eyes.

In her performance she tried to express what she felt for him, equalling his passion and reserve and adding her excitement at the breathtaking vividness of life.

She chose the Waldstein sonata. On the day of the concert there were two performances, one in the afternoon and one in the evening for parents. What had been a private need now became a shared reality. Her face was shining with pleasure. Before she started she'd noted where he sat and when she finished she searched out his face.

He had his head turned away but when he looked at her she saw what looked like anger, even contempt. She couldn't believe it and looked at other faces - some were happy, pleased with her. She looked at the staff - they were very pleased, the Maths mistress was standing and clapping - "You're a dark horse." she said afterwards - but for Molly it wasn't enough. Her hands and legs were still trembling and more and more it registered her anxiety.

When she got home and the memory of Tom's face came back it wouldn't leave. At the evening performance she sat at the piano quaking with fright and sick with disgust - she played accurately and defensively. Harry was bitterly disappointed.

The sense of failure had triumphed. She saw herself fat and fiercely obsessed with something no-one wanted.

13

When Molly reached the sixth form she expected to be able to work in an adult way - to her this meant staff and pupils sharing their enthusiasm for the subject. She saw herself as having leapt the age gap - she'd never been able to accept the barrier anyway - and felt the staff must by now be equally convinced it didn't exist, but the radical change she'd been looking for wasn't on offer. Teachers walked into the small intimate sixth-form room with obvious relief. The middle-aged English mistress marked the transition by sitting girlishly on the edge of the table swinging her legs. She smiled round at the boys and made more references to the erotic in her texts. She slipped back to sixteen rather than moving them up towards thirty-five. Molly's need for an excited interchange of ideas was met by a playful pussy-cuff of words. The Latin master, who'd been ill, turned up late, slumped into the seat in front of them, started his best pupil off on the next section of Virgil's Aeneid and slowly - resisting each slip of his body into the depths, his face going pale and faintly green - fell asleep. The History teacher read out her college notes, never pausing for question, and wound up with a college essay topic for their homework. She left the room bright-eyed and satisfied.

But it was the music lessons that disappointed her most. Her one consolation was that she was the only student taking it at A Level and the chats with the music master were therefore along the lines she wanted. He left her to work alone and that pleased her but for energy and excitement she had to look to herself. After the first sixth months it began to have a bad effect. She sat at the piano tinkering not playing and ended up reading musical biography or listening to records. Frustrated, lonely, she didn't know whether the cause was inside or out.

The truly exciting aspect of the year was the presence of Tom Parsons, not in lessons, he was in the second year sixth, but in the classroom at break times. She stayed in the form room on the off-chance he'd come in for something. Head propped on elbows over a book, next to the radiator she'd named 'the sleeper,' she waited.

He'd placed her on his dinner table, being Head Boy in charge of the layout and Molly took her place next to him but wouldn't talk. A boy from her year sat on the other side of him and the two talked politics and religion. The discussions weren't interesting - David Parkes was slight, blond-haired, blond-skinned and a religious bigot. He'd pause, raising invisible eyebrows before answering Tom's crudely provocative questions. During the verbal ping-pong that followed Tom seemed to enjoy himself while eating and gave the occasional glance at Molly to join in. She chewed fast, secretly and stared out of the window. The compulsiveness of her behaviour and her pale face seemed to fascinate him. They hardly ever exchanged words.

At the end of the autumn term both she and Tom had small parts in the school production of *As You Like It*. The rehearsals bored her because no-one, including herself, cared how it sounded or looked. They fooled around as much on stage as off, only more self-consciously. The dress rehearsals and performances were different - dressed up and with make-up they were excited at their new selves and the quality of the performance leapt up. Molly had about seven lines at the end of the play as Hymen and in Greek clothing, her dark hair in a filet, she was pleased with the effect. Representing the goddess of marriage was a tonic to her again jaded sexual confidence.

Tom had an equally small part as 'the youngest son of old Sir Roland de Bois' but he'd been lovingly allocated the most stunning suit by the English mistress directing the play. He strode on to the stage dressed in purple delivering his lines as if his person were the culmination of the performance - which to Molly it was. She often went back to the stage afterwards when the table and chairs for morning assembly were on it, to recapture some of the excitement and passion she'd experienced in the wings.

One Saturday she went to a rugby match to watch him play and arrived late because she couldn't find the field. She got her first view of the game as he was hurling himself over the goal line. The warming up process long over and the players at their best, she grew excited at the whole spectacle and especially at being committed to one side, but the reason for it took over and soon she saw only Tom's energetic attack - his hurtling grab at another player's legs, the sudden bursts of speed and fleshy violence of head and shoulders. She went away holding the experience as if it were too much to carry. But again the excitement faded because Tom was only marginally aware of her. A positive was that after an experience of this kind she took the energy back to her work and felt she knew what she and it were about. That too faded and she went back to her brooding.

There was only one event that year, unconnected with Tom, that made a lasting impression - her class's visit to a performance of *Coriolanus*. From the beginning she was caught by Coriolanus's passion for achievement, the power of the mother and his inability to bring intensity into line with the requirements of others. Outraged by the mother and the system, she loathed his subjugation to both and him for giving himself to them - but the power of it never left her.

On the way home in the bus she was still stunned, reliving it. The English teacher asked if she'd liked it and dismissed her words of passionate admiration with a touch of contempt. Molly had freak and unreliable tastes in literature, she thought, and was obstinate with it.

"Come on," she said, "it's not one of his best."

Next day at home Molly was still brooding. Harry asked how she'd got on with it.

"Terrific!" - and she was ready to leave it at that but he made one more move:

"I don't think I've ever read it or heard it - not supposed to be one of his best, is it?"

"It was the best play I've ever seen!"

"Why? - what's it about?"

She told the story briefly, growing angry that Coriolanus had to show his scars, and as she described his downfall she lost control and burst into tears:

"What right had she - filling him up with that crap of excellence and death! She separated him so there was nothing but her and what she stood for. I was so pleased when he went over to the other side. She was much more dangerous than him. The glory, the achievement were hers! She valued him only as he fulfilled her expectations. As a person he didn't exist - neither did she, because her power and self-respect came from the codes she operated. When he was a free-ranging force and a threat she broke him."

Harry couldn't make her out. "I don't see what you mean - from what you say he was an arrogant sod going against his own people out of vanity."

"Out of *her* vanity, you fool!" she shouted, then simmering down: "He couldn't see anything but the achievement - if you sacrifice everything to it, it becomes its own justification and has its own momentum."

"You can't blame her for that!"

"The way she breaks him means she knows what she's done, knows she's set him up. It's herself who's to be the ultimate principle. She goes down on her knees to him" - Molly began to cry with pity and fury - "and he's so confused, so distressed he gives her back his life, everything. Wipes everything out as if he'd never been."

"Molly, Molly!"- Harry was shocked and angry - "what's got into you? You've got it all upside down."

Molly was ill in the night, her gastric trouble returned promising a long stay and was one of the most violent and prolonged attacks she'd had. It showed no signs of easing in the following month and she spent more time at home than at school under a covering note that called it gastroenteritis. The depression that went with it was more hateful than the illness. She felt separate from her parents but still couldn't sleep except with her mother and still needed to drag her along to concerts and cinemas as a buffer between herself and the world.

Louise didn't mind too much. She lived quite a vigorous life dividing her interests between home and work and Molly was jealous of her outside world. She wanted that freedom for herself but couldn't get it. She half blamed Louise for her own inability which resulted in a kind of resentment that labelled her sharp talk and coarse jokes "vulgar," though she loved them, and when Louise fell asleep from boredom during a concert she raged at being tied to someone so indifferent to what set her afire.

At the same time she couldn't feel easy with Harry. When he wanted to talk she wouldn't. When she did talk it was likely to be about men, sex, pop music, cinema - anything he hated. It would have been easy to revert to her old pattern, sharing one interest with him, the other with Louise, but she couldn't. She wouldn't have Louise's version of sex or Harry's of culture.

She moped at home and faded into the background at school. Games were a torment, especially with her weak gut. Her reluctance and ineffectuality were put down to fatness rather than boredom and ill-health but she didn't care. Moving about the school or at home was an effort, she wanted to sprawl - in an armchair or in her desk - she only walked when it was unavoidable: movement made her feel sick and her legs felt lined with lead. Her sick appearance added to her suffering. She loathed her unhealthy face.

She felt her cause with Tom Parsons was hopeless and it made her spiteful. Once when he asked her to play the piano in morning assembly she refused snappily. He was annoyed and looked at her slumped against the radiator. Her book was open and he flipped it shut.

"Less of that and more fresh air. You live in your emotions. Don't you ever need exercise? You're too tense and neurotic; why don't you do something about it?"

Molly was speechless with rage and took up the book. He snatched it. She pulled it to her. He tried to peel her hands off. She leapt up in the desk, banging the lid and hurting her hip but put the book behind her back and he was forced to reach round for it. At the closeness of their bodies they both stopped - he with an air of embarrassed contempt, she with sudden terror she'd been betrayed.

"How dare you tell me what's good for me, how dare you think you know what I need!" She paused but couldn't stop - wanting to hurt him: "*Your* needs might be simply satisfied - mine aren't!"

He looked amused. "What pleasure can you get from a radiator? Why don't you read outside? - I do! Why do you make yourself unhealthy?"

"I don't *make* myself, you idiot! And anyway, how do you know what pleasure I get from the radiator? I love its smell - warm and relaxing - dirt and paint - lovely fug!" She put her hand behind her to touch it and sat down opening the book but glancing up to see if he were going.

He was still there looking flushed, amused and intensely curious.

14

Molly's second year in the sixth form was more miserable than the first. Tom had left for Cambridge and her own preparation for A Levels and possible entrance to a music college was a nightmare. The work was tiring, limited and left no time for exploration - any spontaneous interest was a threat to success and unbalanced the programme. She was useless at exams, the necessary tailoring bored and irritated her. Scraping through would do and she decided not to work towards anything else. With her bowels sick more often than well she continuously had that feeling of suspended life that had been the worst feature of the previous year.

When she got the required A Levels and was offered a place at the Royal College of Music she still wasn't pleased. She'd had enough. The last two years at school had drained her and several weeks after the end of her last term Molly told her parents she wasn't going:

"I can't stand any more of it! All I want is to play the piano."

Harry argued she'd never play if she didn't go through the right channels: "You've still so much to learn - you think you know it all. They'll never take you seriously."

She believed the last bit but was adamant. She wanted to find things out for herself - above all to move outside the confines of home and school. She took a job as waitress in George's father's cafe - the family was back from America with more money and this was a new acquisition - they already had a lumber yard and grocer's. Mary, Rose's sister, thought her husband had over-extended himself but though she'd resisted him every foot of the way had blossomed into a portly prototype of middleclass affluence. George had liked the projects from the beginning and enjoyed acting as sub-manager at each place in turn.

Molly occasionally worked at the grocer's shop but preferred the cafe. She dressed extravagantly - "like a Woolworth's tart," Harry told her - but the more abusive he was the more obstinately she clung to her new style. She became a stout charmer in the cafe - much in demand. Her nickname was "Sunshine." The work was hot and boring in itself but she hardy noticed it. All her attention was for the people, especially the men. One regular customer, George said, was recently out of prison - a middle-aged well-dressed man more healthy and alive than most. She was greatly excited by the attention he paid her and when he took both her hands and held them saying, "You make my day, Sunshine!" she was amazed it didn't matter that he didn't mean it. Even so she refused to meet him after work and got George to take her home in the car.

The excitement of her new role and renewed interest in people - above all in the eternal erotic daydreaming - might have faded if her relationship with George hadn't picked up again. It took some time because when Molly started the job he'd been engaged to be married. It gave them pause for a few weeks but proximity and the change in her manner were too much for both of them. Molly found him more attractive than ever. He'd grown tall and his fatness had gone except for a little around the face where it made a sensual setting for the smile and bright eyes. Buttering rolls together, huddled close in a small area partitioned off for preparing snacks, they were only just separated from kitchen and cafe and the potential exposure was exciting. A quick kiss could lengthen into a sensual discovery and make both of them lose consciousness long enough for a sharp clack from the kitchen door to fling them apart as if shot.

When George got married Molly was a bridesmaid and had her dress made up by the wife of his best friend. The friend, Malcolm, was often home on the evenings Molly went for fittings. Her experience with George had relaxed her, she leant less heavily on make-up and earrings and in spite of working with food had lost a little weight - she was looking younger and more alive. For the first couple of evenings Malcolm watched her closely, absorbed by her lively chatter and fascinated by the way she crossed her legs. Then after a fortnight she accidentally met him at the top of the stairs on her way to the bathroom. Flushed, bright-eyed, saying something she couldn't understand - his mouth seemed blocked by his tongue - she felt his hand tremble as he put it to her face and moved into his arms at the instant he put them round her.

From this point, with two men, she was happy. Alive to every male face, appreciative of every sinewy arm and tight buttock, the world was glorious - male beauty was everywhere and the only riches. Each caress was more than an adventure - it was the culmination and meaning of all other adventure. But eventually even this palled. With no stable or permanent contact she began to sadden again and in time the gastric trouble returned and the old pallor and moodiness.

Eight months in the cafe were enough. She needed to be focussed and returned to her music with new intensity but still wasn't ready to consider college. Instead she accepted stand-in music jobs in local schools and at one of them a sudden death left a vacancy she was asked to fill till other arrangements could be made. After two terms no other teacher had been found and Molly was reasonably content to let things ride, finding she enjoyed teaching other subjects besides music - in fact preferred it. In music lessons her own interest took over, forcing the pace and making her lose touch with the class. Only when she played to them did it satisfy them both - the class quite liked being taken over by sound and outmatched in volume. The music room was next to the cookery room, both housed in a wing of their own - persistent and acrimonious complaints came from the cookery teacher which she felt able to ignore.

Other subjects woke old interests - she enjoyed the children's natures, loved their poor acting in plays and their readiness to invent. In maths the majority of them worked with patient drudgery - disappearing occasionally behind desk lids for a break, as she had. Sympathising with how they felt made discipline no great strain but in music lessons she sometimes had trouble.

Teaching was tiring. She came home in the evening not wanting to do more than watch television - Louise had rented one and it had been accepted with very little protest from Harry. All three women had been prepared to do battle and he knew it but in recompense they deferred to his occasional requests. Sometimes from his hideout in the other room he'd pop his head round the door, tense with irritation, to ask them to turn down the sound. Westerns were the worst. He found himself waiting for gunshots and drum music and it drove him wild.

Even so Molly saw him as more patient as well as more withdrawn. In fact he was glad to have the three women in another room - the different strains of their company were becoming too much. Molly worried and puzzled him. She'd lost the direction and energy he'd thought unchangeable and he tried to prevent himself feeling bitter or spiteful about the ordinary female she'd become. Mistrust caused increasing strain between them because Molly detected inflexions of contempt or dismissal before he'd fully thought them.

The "television room" as he bitterly called the sittin-groom provided other strains as well. The compassionate revulsion he felt at the sight and smell of his old mother was beginning to worry him. Ruth had aged rapidly and become incontinent. She gave off a stink of urine at all times no matter how often she changed her knickers and the old woman couldn't be turned away from the electric fire even in warm weather. For him the suffocation and airless heat, the sight of her legs sprawled apart with mottle burns glowing through the stockings as she watched television or snored faintly produced a disgust he was ashamed of. Molly and Louise seemed unshaken by it. Nothing stirred Molly from the box and Louise was happier than she'd ever been - she seemed to enjoy and understand Molly at last. He could hear them shrieking with laughter together.

Waiting for things to change he was happiest keeping his distance or going back to them when he felt like it, and when they watched a programme of his choice he felt his old mastery undiminished. One thing hadn't altered - Molly could be made to talk about anything they'd watched together with very little prompting but they both had axes to grind and the whirring came through the mildest discussions.

Molly sometimes went to the cinema with a friend she'd made at school - a young unmarried teacher whose inter-ests, like hers, were primarily outside the institution. Once or twice she went to a local dance with her, and here she met a man she saw regularly for a while.

Ten years older than herself, Jack had separated from his wife. He was an ex-guardsman of a breadth and height that satisfied even Molly's increasing notions of the world-oblit-erating proportions of man. This was the first time she'd been able to enjoy trips with a boyfriend and they went to shows and concerts together. Once or twice in the past it had worried her that men who were relaxed enough to want her were either married or about to be. With each of them she'd kept her full nature in check, especially as circumstances left no time for any exchange but the sexual.

With Jack there was more time and for a while Molly felt perky. She liked being diminished by bulk, liked looking round the West End with new confidence and security. His sexual demands weren't more than she felt able to satisfy. He had, he said, a reverence for her virginity and this put her at ease for as long as she believed it. She wasn't able to think realistically about love-making but knew that for her the problem wasn't one of eagerness. The intensity of her interests and excitements worked against the kind of relationship she wanted and she dreamed of a man who wouldn't be shocked, worn out or offended by the things she said or was or the demands she seemed to make.

15

Discontented with her relationship with Jack she kept it going because it had elements of life in it. They didn't talk much. When she was over-moved by a film he patted her hand. She liked the protection and solace but he eyed her as if she were odd. The length of time it took to get over a disturbing film - the seriousness with which she took it - rather amused him and she got cross when he found her the better entertainment. Sometimes she'd talk it over with Harry - more often she'd re-create a balance by playing.

She got thinner, restless. Her slimness enabled her to wear fashionable clothes which she chose not to suit her looks but to satisfy a new feeling of being a sophisticate because of her relationships with married men. Out of school hours, when not too battered by the day's work, she gave the impression of being a well-dressed haughty young woman, and it was on one such occasion she met Tom Parsons again. They'd not seen each other for nearly two years.

Molly was waiting to get off a bus and shifted aside to allow room for a passenger coming downstairs. She was shocked to see him. A quaking wateriness at the knees made her grip the rail and she stared with amazed radiance into Tom's face. He reddened and smiled. When they were both off they exchanged questions. Molly tried to get together her recently acquired sophistication. Desperate to break through the mental paralysis caused by his good looks she released only a gas of giggles floating up meaningless answers.

Tom was piqued trying to make out what was different about her apart from the fact she was slimmer. It came to him. The way she stood, her clothes and something about her manner in spite of the giggles convinced him suddenly she was a very sexual woman. He became excited. Within the next few minutes he'd arranged a meeting at the Tate Gallery for the following Saturday.

For the rest of the working week Molly was changed towards children and staff alike - every activity was life and its pulse raced with hers.

On Saturday it was cool and overcast and Tom was buttoned and belted into a raincoat. He smiled and put his hand under her elbow going up the steps. Inside, the gallery was stuffy and Molly followed him to the room of his choice, relieved to have paintings to stare at. The filtered light, subdued sounds and smell of polish conflicted with the life on the walls. She was confused and ready to leave till the amazing energy of the pictures broke through. They were in the Impressionists room - most of them she'd never seen before. She began to stand for long spells in front of them, leaning over the rope for closer inspection. In another room she stared at portraits with the same intensity of absorption she watched people. The peering and the time it took began to irritate Tom:

"You're supposed to look from a distance and get it in perspective."

Molly blushed at the disapproval that reminded her of the concert. "I don't want the perspective!"

"Well, you can't get inside!" There was distaste in his voice.

Seeing his back a few pictures down, the craving to be close made her want to explain and she came up behind him. "I'm not trying to get inside but behind," she said mildly - "see what he saw, what drove him."

Tom frowned with a faint smile. She ventured to take his arm - he let it rest but she felt a stiffening and couldn't tell if it were the intimacy or leftover irritation. She left her hand where it was and removed it in her own good time to walk off and look at something else but there was a growing feeling of self-disgust and she was surprised to see him follow her and start up again:

"It's the organised whole that matters. It's what the painter makes of what drove him. Balance, proportion, colour make it meaningful - that's his achievement."

"Those are his tools!" She was angry now and decided on the instant the whole thing was hopeless, blushing as she remembered the string of girls he'd gone out with in his last year at school. She didn't fit and she turned to tell him they'd separate and meet up in the cafe - when she saw his face was red and shining and that he'd undone his coat.

"Shall we get a drink?"

Molly half ran down the stairs with him. He fetched tea and a cake - still looking bright and happy. Finally he took off his coat and dropped it on a spare seat.

"What have you been doing with yourself - apart from teaching?" he asked.

"Working in a cafe."

He raised his eyebrows. "How long?"

"About six months."

"Why?"

"Felt like it."

"Enjoy it?"

Very much." Something in the way she said it excited him.

"Why?"

"My cousin runs the place - we had a good time." The following silence was hard for him to break.

"Get on well with your cousin?"

"He's very attractive."

Tom blushed. "How many men have you been out with since you left school?"

"A few!"

He studied her fingers round the cup then rummaged in his pocket for a tin, opening it and showing several han-drolled cigarettes. The tin was shaking as he offered it and the cigarettes rolled around. Molly took one, hardly able to believe her eyes. The quaking match that followed left no doubt and she grew more confident. They kept away from opinions for the rest of the day and drew closer.

Two weeks after the visit Molly went down to Cambridge. Tom met her at the station and in a businesslike, proprietary way took her back to his rooms.

"You can make us an omelette if you like," he told her.

She was resentful at having to show her domestic paces, especially as she'd never made one. The room was hot. He frightened her by referring to the scarlet spreadeagled tulips in his vase:

"I want you to open like that!"

The idea that he meant sexually, as if the rest didn't matter, tightened her up. Straightforwardness in his physical priorities had been one of the excitements - now it was a threat. He kissed her and she felt nothing, though when he moved away she found herself quaking and longing. Her guard stayed up for the rest of the day but her excitement was so intense she couldn't eat - he ate both their suppers.

When he saw her to the station in the evening he wrapped his scarf round her neck and she wore it home. It stayed round her, indoors and out, for the rest of the weekend.

Louise, intrigued by the scarf, questioned Molly about him: "What's he like?"

"Handsome, brilliant - you remember how well he did at school?"

"Oh, that one! - conceited sod he looked to me."

When Molly mentioned Tom casually to Harry, Louise glanced at the scarf round Molly's neck and pulled a face behind her back.

Molly had invited Tom to her house during the following weekend. Louise was keen to get a glimpse of him again and make up her mind. He arrived on Saturday morning, smiled affably and shook hands, staring round the room and at Louise while she chatted. She felt he was studying her - indifferently amused. After a while she grew flustered and irritable while he grew more at ease. He took off his sports jacket and flung it in a chair to lounge back in his own more comfortably. Molly thought his easy body was magnificent. The shirt held it tightly and clung when he moved.

He left in the early evening and Molly asked what she'd been burning to: "What did you think of him?"

Louise was bent to one of the cupboards and straightened up keeping her back to her.

"Mum!"

"Yes, I heard," then turning, "he's not *my* kind!" she said.

It amazed and hurt Molly more than she could have imagined. She'd long given up expecting them to think alike about most things but about this she'd been confident. "Why?"

"I wouldn't want him."

"Why not?"

"I just wouldn't."

"Don't you think he's handsome?"

Louise shrugged. "Some might."

"What've you got against him?"

"Thinks too bloody much of himself. Looks straight through you!"

"Is that all! Dad does that when he wants to."

"Don't compare him with your father. Dad's brainy without thinking everyone's a funny-looking object."

Molly left and went upstairs, not to sleep but to lie awake and fume. Tom was different and she liked the difference. Her father had patronised Louise so much she must be looking for it.

The following morning Louise ventured a little more: "He'd give you a tough life - push you around mercilessly."

She stared at her mother. "He might *try*. You worry about *yourself!*"

Seeing she was angry Louise wanted to make peace, especially as Harry was coming down the corridor: "Okay, p'raps you're right."

On Sunday Molly played to Tom all morning while Louise cooked a big meal. Ruth got in the way, peeling, washing vegetables and stacking plates - she'd rather have done the lot herself. The family was mostly silent through lunch. Harry asked questions about Cambridge and Tom answered without interest but told him he had thought of chucking it all in and joining the Merchant Navy. He postponed the decision, he said, after telling his father, who'd had a breakdown and begged him to stay at least to the end of the year. Molly looked at Louise to see what she made of that but there were no signs of a changing attitude.

"Isn't Molly's playing magnificent!" Tom said suddenly looking first at Louise then at Harry.

Harry smiled - eyes widening and lightening. His universally friendly manner had welcomed Tom from the start and from the start Tom had liked him.

"Can't you persuade her to take up her place at the Royal College?" Tom asked.

"I've never known why she didn't!"

Tom looked at Molly with such reproach and intimacy she was overjoyed - beaming with happiness at both of them without answering.

In the afternoon Molly took Tom for a walk through the local woods. Most of the tension between them had gone. She talked about her reasons for not taking her place and about ill health and the frustrated activity that seemed a natural part of her life.

"I could never make you out in the sixth form," he said, confident he could now.

She asked why he'd seemed so critical of her. He denied

110

it:

"I always felt curious, even roused against my will."

"Thanks!"

"I don't know why - sort of schoolboy funk - and you weren't pretty in the ordinary way!"- he put his arm round her and drew her closer - "I probably loved you even then."

Molly stopped to examine his face. He looked strained and embarrassed.

"No you didn't - I'd have known. Anyway you were going out with Mary Travers and Betty Marsden."

"I was watching you." A distortion of discomfort in his face made her think he might mean it.

"Mary told me about your kisses and what you did."

"So what!"

"Why didn't you kiss me? I'd have given anything!"

"I wasn't sure what you were like. You didn't seem sexy and your playing -"

"What about my playing? - why did you pull a face when I played in the concert?"

He looked bewildered.

"I was playing for you, and you looked contemptuous and dismissive."

Tom blushed. "I was very moved."

"You didn't look it."

"I was! I think I resented being moved. You seemed so spiritual - given to the music - bodiless."

"Couldn't you tell it wasn't like that - didn't it make you feel alive?"

"That was the music."

"But if I'd played it dead you'd have felt it dead."

"Perhaps." He smiled and tightened his grip.

They spent some time in silence, handling the leaves, following each other down tracks till Molly suddenly

111

stopped and Tom came up to kiss her. This time she responded so much she clung to him to keep upright - silently begging for endless kisses, never having enough - but Tom wanted to go further and still she couldn't.

He decided to stay over for the Monday and they planned a trip to Kew Gardens and a picnic there.

It was late May, sunny but not too hot. They wandered round the grounds talking, touching, sitting under trees. Molly lay between him and a rough trunk, entranced with both. They walked between rhododendron bushes blazing with colour. A melting and transforming sun focussed her on fierce insect activity - heady pollen - children running - an irritable mother with an abstracted father pushing a squeaky chair - metal against petal - hair moving like leaves in a lymph of light blending skin with tarmac in an inter-flowing that left Molly breathless.

They stood by a circular pond full of gold and flesh-pink fish looking naked in shade but in sunlight shafting a brilliance unmatchable. A snout broke through the surface - its sensuality like sexual awakening.

In the hothouses Tom let go her hand. They moved down narrow passageways squeezing between people, towering fleshy leaves and hanging flowers. Instead of slowing the pace down the heat exaggerated it - she was taken over by the breath and weight and luxuriance of another life. The sun beat through the glass till she panicked she'd faint.

Tom refused to go into any more, his face looked blotchy and Molly's dangerously pale.

Towards the evening she suggested going back to a London park and listening to a band. He didn't want to - a concert or a play would have been different - but in Hyde Park listening to the band and watching her eagerness for handsome healthy faces and energetic trumpets Tom was partly satisfied. He studied others in deck chairs and on the grass, took in the city round them and in spite of his determination to stay free felt freer with her than on his own. He'd wanted to bed all the women he clapped eyes on and a niggling resentment made him scrutinise the girls around him. He didn't want to enough.

16

Their wedding took place in August.

Two days before it Tom turned up with a stranger he introduced as Graham, his best man. They'd come to tell the family they were going to collect the wedding cake from the baker's.

Louise was tense and already lonely, unable to imagine life without Molly. Harry'd been over-busy with assurances but none had worked, either on her or himself. He reasoned with her and with his feelings till he achieved a pale-faced eagerness and brightness of manner that delighted Molly and made Louise feel perhaps after all it would be alright if they lived close. She'd achieved a balance with Molly in the old life but Tom might never let her have a footing in the new - every day brought new shocks and now the lordly young men were on the doorstep assuming a right to do something spontaneously she'd carefully set aside the time for. She'd ordered the cake, chosen the design and bought it - she had the right to bring it home!

She attacked as soon as they told her. Graham was amazed at the ferocity of the tense, lined face, putting up with it only by letting it pass and reach what he considered to be the proper target. He stood to one side, face congested, unnerved and furious at her for ignoring his vulnerability as a stranger.

The rightful target appeared not to notice. He repeated they'd go now and told Louise reassuringly they had a suitable container with handles to bring it back in. His impassiveness irritated even Molly but allayed her anxiety. She saw her mother unable to keep going in the face of it. It was as if he were simpleminded - no tense determination, anger or vengeful obstinacy. Molly was as confused as Louise.

Tom and Graham left and having brought back the cake left again and Louise, who'd been biting her tongue, ventured the abnormally mild comment, "Can't make head or tail of him." She pulled her mouth down more in disparagement than contempt.

Molly thought it the most successful way of getting your own way she'd ever seen - he just switched off. She was dealing with a personality she didn't understand. The inaccessibility frightened her but gave her space.

Louise bought a new dress for the occasion and took pleasure in the formal aspects of the wedding. Harry constantly exchanged encouraging, loving words with Molly but she noticed he looked a lot older.

"Isn't life exciting!" she said, "I love you so much yet I'm dying to go."

He smiled with genuine approval. In general Molly felt happy about her parents and any reservations were put behind her.

On the morning of the day the first person she saw was Mike. He barged into the kitchen while she was leaning over the sink fussing with her hair. His face alight with excitement, brown eyes searching hers with the same glee as when she was a child - he wanted some fun.

"Hop it, Uncle, you're not supposed to chivvy a girl on her wedding morning!"

"Chivvy? - me? I wanted to see the blushing bride and give her a kiss for the last time before she belonged to someone else."

"Honestly! - anyone would think I was going abroad or wouldn't love anyone ever again." She kissed him heartily. "I hope everyone got up next door? You mustn't be late."

"The boys are up and Rose has been fiddling since seven. What are you going to do, Moll? Have you decided?"

"What about?"

"Tom's got another year at Cambridge."

"Dad didn't tell you? I'm taking my place at college in September - heard officially the other day."

Goose-hollows appeared. "Harry's pleased, I bet!"

"I can't wait to go either, that's the daft thing. I'm full of Tom and my future."

"Wonderful!"

"Then why suddenly look sad?"

"I don't know, other people's happiness makes me feel sad sometimes - left out, I suppose."

Molly threw her arms round his neck with as much abandon as when she was a child. "How could you ever be left out of anything that ever happens to me? What about when you come to my concerts! Think how intimate we'll be then - closer than ever."

He looked puzzled then suddenly radiant.

Half an hour later a card written in pencil came through the letterbox, hand-delivered by Tom:

"Darling Molly, I shan't see you till we're married and

then I shan't really see you, I'll be poker stiff with fright and desire, and after that..." There wasn't any more.

Quaking with excitement, Molly went through the rest of her preparations half conscious. People came in and out, asked questions and got answers while she stared at her darlings with liquid-eyed radiance.

A WOMAN'S MAN

1

Winifred was standing in the middle of the room with a glass of sherry raised in one hand - the other supporting her elbow. She was tense and the stomach-hugging position made her lean over in an anxious, assertive way, but happy excitement was obvious underneath. John watched her - she was completely involved in the conversation with her supervisor and the strains of that relationship. John was one of the two third-years invited to a postgraduate party - the other was being shepherded in at this moment and directed towards him. The professor's gentle wife never stopped smiling, nodding and raising her eyebrows in interest at the newcomer's remarks till she'd delivered him.

"What've they got to drink?" Paul asked in a stage whisper before she was out of earshot and she came back with a glass of wine. John had mixed feelings about his friend. At the moment he was irritated at Paul's need not just to feel at home but have his feet up - control and ease were top priorities that sacrificed other people's without noticing. Sometimes he admired both but found them crossing his own path too often to make him a close friend.

Only one other, a middleaged tutor, had turned up in a

suit but Paul rightly assumed his nature gave a more convincing show of informality than jeans did for the others, while leaving him free to dress up. His expression and his suit let them all know he might look like a farmer - healthy, strong-bodied, active - but it was an intellectual crop he was after. He picked up John's respectful appraisal which increased his confidence to the point where he had to express it. He found a pretty face, his tutor's wife's, and eyed it. The only thing spoiling his fun was the sound of Winifred's voice raised above the others. He wondered what on earth John saw in her - body thin as a blade and a cutting tone to go with it. He was sick of hearing she was interesting and he craned forward to see who she was talking to. Smiling, he relaxed back. Robertson looked uncomfortable but not as much as Win, who seemed in two minds whether to dominate or seduce. It was almost touching. Intellect was ridiculous in a sexually untutored female.

The wine made his cheeks blaze and he rocked back on his heels. "She's giving Robertson a rough time!"

John ignored the tone and moved up behind her. He told himself he got more from even her most far-fetched remarks than from anyone else at this place. Excitable responses gave her thinking life. The impassioned obstinacy it sometimes gave rise to didn't always go down well with others. She couldn't find any easy answers and it kept her on edge. Now he was looking at her back, lightly touching it, she recognised the touch and relaxed a little.

Robertson relaxed too. "I was going to say" - smiling at John - "in the last plays Ibsen's making it clear society's against the exceptional, against the ideal in fact. It only wants and tolerates the mediocre."

"Society isn't," Win said, "I wish it were - life is!"

"But in those last plays it's the artists as achievers who

are making the greatest demands on society and can't be forgiven."

"It's not the *demanding* artist that rocks the boat, it's the understanding one."

"Don't the two go together?"

"Yes, but I'm disagreeing with your view of his thinking in those plays. The Master Builder was an egomaniac destroying himself. You're wrong about society - it promotes idealism - it's its main escape route. Dazzle and blind yourself with the ideal and you're spared thinking about the actual. Over-simplify what may look desirable till it becomes impossible and an outrage to life, then you can pay it lip-service as the goal no-one's strong, good or wise enough to achieve. Ideals are thought-inhibitors and whatever inhibits thought is useful to society. They're convenience products, expensive at one level but inexpensive of time and effort - and with such a low nourishment level."

"What about writers like Shakespeare and Tolstoy? - they demand more from their readers than anyone."

"They don't *demand* anything. They appeal to the growing centre of us all - however small that is. They don't make crusades but try to achieve a balance and take their readers as far as they can." She'd stopped looking at him and was staring miserably at a point behind him and to the right.

John, feeling she needed comfort, put his arm round her waist and she leant gratefully. It was the cue.

"We'll finish this Thursday fortnight," Robertson said breezily and moved off towards a commanding middle-aged woman shouting playfully at him, "Harold, you're a bad boy!" He put his hand across his breast in playful apology and slipped happily into the conversation of her group.

Winifred wasn't ready to give up yet. She'd recovered her spirits and started searching faces.

"Don't let's stay too long." John wanted to get her away.

"Not long. One more drink!"

While he fetched her one she found a chair. She was tireder than she thought. No use hanging around. If they all got drunk it'd be fun. None of it was any good for talking. They might go back to John's room and listen to music. When he came back she put the suggestion he'd been waiting for.

They stayed nearly an hour afterwards just the same, leaning towards each other watching the faces they knew and exchanging comments on what they thought was going on in them. She liked it better than he did - it was a way of joining in.

They walked back to John's room in college - he was humming snatches of the music he wanted to put on.

Indoors, coat on but undone, she sat in the largest armchair so he couldn't easily reach her and waited. Involved, close-knit, brilliantly articulate, the Schubert took her over and when it was finished she looked round for the rest to live up to it.

John was watching her and seeing her move into her own world sat on the floor resting against her legs. His back was exciting and she ran her hand over it, pressing and enjoying its warm energy. She remembered with shame how she'd interpreted his passion for Bach as affectation. She'd hated Bach - still did to some extent - and felt that for him it had been a Cambridge credential like the prints on his walls. When he'd persisted, trying again and again to make her listen, her resistance had broken. She admired him for discovering what she'd been too arrogant and impatient to discover for herself. The experience stayed as if she'd been influenced more subtly and long-lastingly than by a person - a revelation in which he'd been revealed. The gentleness and patience he'd shown her arrogance shamed her again and so much it quickly turned to longing. She was still puzzled on occasions by the dull expression of his life in speech but mostly ignored it, mistrusting her judgment - his hesitancy was more valuable than her hotheadedness. The touch of complacency she sometimes saw wasn't there with her.

A kiss on her knee brought her back and she slipped to the floor putting her mouth up to be kissed. His tongue roused her so much their bodies' separation - he hadn't put his arms round her - became painful and she put her arms round his neck, moving closer. He didn't move. In a while she stood up aching with desire and saw his pale face submerged in sensation but with no suggestion of action. She was nearly in tears.

"I've got to go."

He stood up obediently and walked her back - their arms round each other and Win chatting about the music. Easing distress through talk was habitual to her and she got excited about the quartet. There was a high wall in front of the four-storied house where she had a room. A magnificent plane tree extended two heavy arms from behind it. In daylight the opening leaves were convulsing with life - at night the soft shapes looked fully achieved. She became unexpectedly angry at John's reverential handling of them and went indoors barely muttering goodnight.

2

The following morning was Saturday and she woke tired, dressing slowly and putting on the same skirt and jumper she'd worn for a fortnight. The smell of the jumper was too much and she flung it across the room, shivering while she searched through her drawers for a new one. She'd bought it several weeks ago and hadn't worn it because of the colour. After throwing everything on the bed her irritable thoroughness paid off and she found it jammed between the drawer and back of the chest and put it on without further thought, though the pale mauve looked as hostile as it had six weeks before.

Having arranged to meet John at the boathouse she walked there after a quick coffee, intending to be first. Her coat was open and shivering all the way she began to get excited. The wind soughed through the branches of the trees by the river and she sat on the boathouse steps trembling and covering her knees. All sense of time disappeared in watching. Beating wings, scudding feet - excited ducks on the dark water - their fierceness and sudden rawthroated sounds blotting out everything else. A drake landed like a light blow on the back of a duck. He gripped her neck in his beak and forced it down outstretched on the water. The neck swayed wildly under manic pressure and was abruptly released.

She stood up hearing footsteps on the path at the side of the shed and turned to see John.

"You all right? " he asked.

White faced silence.

"You look distraught."

The experience was destroyed and she grew cross: "I'm not distraught."

"Come on then, wrap up."

Crosser still at the solicitude she sat up in the punt he hired - bright and keen and looking about her, but separate. He took the punt from its moorings and worked into a comfortable rhythm with the pole. Another boatload of punters came up behind them, a male punting two females. He was determined to pass, coming abreast and pretending not to be able to move the weight of the two complacent female bodies. Puffing and grinning he suddenly went into lurches and heaves of the pole till he'd moved on - freeing his face just long enough to wink at Winifred.

Instantly happy she shouted, "Cor!" There was a caressive undercurrent in the mockery that gave extra power to his next push. She lolled back on the cushions and noticed John's irritation. "What a back!" she said spitefully.

"So powerfully dedicated to showing off!" His mouth was pinched with reproachful anger.

"Plenty to show." Her coat fell open and the jumper glowed luminously aggressive.

They were passing a wood where vivid new grass was piercing dead leaves. Some of the smaller trees were in leaf and made a light suspension of green against bare branches. She longed to be in there and noticing her look he drew into the bank, jamming the pole into the mud. His patience with her reversed her feelings again and they walked through the wood cuddling and making up. Win was comforted but unhappy - full of excited responses which began to feel like an illness because they had nowhere to go.

He sensed the repressed intensity and his growing caution in response to it felt to her like increasingly wooden responsiveness. He'd learnt from experience that attempts to make things better could make them worse, so without question on his part or confession on hers they planned the rest of their day. It included a trip to the cinema - always a success with Winifred.

In the early evening the film had worked its usual magic. She came out refreshed -responses to the real world heightened. They sauntered across Parker's Piece watching some boys play football and the ball suddenly rolled to her feet. She kicked energetically and missed, stood back, took another shot and missed again.

"You're no good!" John kicked it smartly to one of the boys in the distance, pleased with himself.

She took his arm. "Smart kicker!" she said.

"Not really. Only by comparison with you."

Having learnt to identify egoism as a form of animal energy, his low key understandng mixed her up. She needed intense excitement, and crude energy often provided it - on the the other hand his honesty seemed closer to the truth than hers. She looked at the aggressive shapes of the boys in the distance kicking a ball no more than a shadow on the darkening grass. Bounding, thumping masses coming heavily together and breaking up into patterns of energy - painfully exciting. She looked at John almost reproachfully. His long pale face and its gleaming nervous energy looked unreal in the twilight. Expression not flesh had the substance. She turned away restless.

"I don't want to go back to your rooms. Let's stay out a bit."

"What about something to eat? - I 'm hungry." He sounded hurt.

"Let's go to the Trojan."

"I'm broke."

She stood still, obstinate. "I don't want to go back. If you want to, go. I want to see people." His face, yellow under the newly lit streetlights, made her more impatient. She walked ahead looking into lighted shop windows.

Crossing the main street she half paused, staring at a young man laughing selfconsciously with his girlfriend. Surely it wasn't that she wanted - no, only the dynamics under it. It suddenly seemed she was looking for that in everything. The darkening evening made her feel concealed and a wild sense of freedom was rising in direct proportion to the increasing weight of confusion and irritation she sensed over her shoulder. She stopped to confront it: eyes full of impatience, manner full of pleading. He took her arm and half pushed her the extra few yards to the Trojan.

Once they were inside they both felt relieved. It was brilliantly lit and familiar. John celebrated by smiling at a darkhaired girl he knew. Winifred had started feeling guilty as soon as she'd got her own way. Suppressing her own instinct to flirt she kept it alive as an exciting promise fed by the noises and light and food smells. They settled at a table. John felt brighter by the second and it made such a difference Winifred reached over to stroke his fingers as he picked up the menu. He took no notice except to close his hand in a sedative way over what he felt to be fretting fingers. He paid attention when he felt them fiercely snatched away and saw her staring tight faced at someone behind him.

Paul was leaning over him. Delighted, John pulled out a chair. "Win was looking for company," he said.

Paul sat next to her while she fidgetted with her knife and fork, wiping them on a tissue in case they weren't properly washed.

"Nice to see you both. Funny how seldom I see the two of you together to talk to. Been enjoying yourselves?"

The remarks, indifferent, unprejudiced and unrelated Win interpreted as a sneer in three parts. His broad hands were resting lightly on the table. In spite of herself she liked them. The full, shining lips expressed the same self-certainty. It was a beauty that needed no-one and she forbade herself to be appreciative. It produced a new tension. She drew herself up and in knocking his knee became excitedly aware of his thighs spread carelessly under the table. At all costs she mustn't touch them again.

"We went to the 'Arts' this afternoon," John said, "saw a good film." He expected to be asked about it but Paul was putting down the menu and trying to catch the waitress's eye. Finally her caught her skirt and put in his order - "And two plain omelettes," John added.

Paul lounged back taking them both in. " It'd do you good to go out with others once in a while like the rest of us" - he winked at Winifred - "if not on your own then as a foursome - it's what life's all about!"

"What is ?"

"Adventure. Other men, other conversation."

"Other men sounds fun."

He grinned. "And the conversation? "

She pulled a face. "You can keep it."

"Not everyone's boring."

"No, only certain people." It came out more pointedly than she wanted and her smile had a sneer in it but he only took note that her teeth were uneven.

He glanced at John, having the same problem as at the party. John sat, legs crossed and to one side as if all this had nothing to do with him.

Win's eyes were filling with tears of frustration and anger.

"Why not try to know people " Paul said to her.

"That's good, coming from you!"

He gave up.

The food arrived and for the most part they ate and ignored each other. Paul and John chatted just enough to ease the tension but Win's small nervous mouthfuls and elbows tucked in kept them both alive to it.

Towards the end of the meal a group of Paul's friends turned up. One of the loudest came over to him, launching instantly into a bantering conversation on the morning lecture. Paul excused himself, taking his coffee and leaving his dessert.

Alone Win found John staring at her, eyebrows raised and mouth compressed to a slit. She looked back at him - half bored, half defiant.

"Enjoy your little scene? " he asked.

"Yep!" It was too late to redeem the situation. What a hateful nuisance Paul was! It wasn't enough for him to be what he was - he had to recruit John. The friendship between them was strange. John didn't care or perhaps didn't notice when Paul patronised him. He seemed half to believe in Paul's tricks. He didn't attend the macho club but still paid a subscription.

She started listening to Paul's loud friend now seated and leaning back from his steak and kidney and punctuating the air with his fork. Someone else was also talking but only the fork was audible:

"He's a stuffy old sod. In fact that writer's good - loves words and knows how to use 'em."

"Needs more than that." The comment came from a sensitive face and nobody noticed. Another face was alive with mischief, partly engaged in the discussion, partly intent on keeping the fork in action, but Paul broke in, slapping down his cup:

"What about Chapman ...." and launched into his opinion of a rising modern novelist. He gave his author his marks out of ten and looked round for corroboration. The sensitive was about to give it but the fork was too quick:

"I hate 'nice' guys facing life and tragedy with basic human dignity and a sense of humour."

Paul laughed too loud.

The uneasy entertainment was over for Win and she slumped into depression, turning her eyes away from the bubbles of saliva at the corners of the next speaker's mouth and manically fighting off the sound of his voice.

She was tired of her life at Cambridge. So many egos and so little energy left over. In the empty vessels of limited writers they could carry their own cargos. Excitement for the challenging stuff was thin on the ground. John was so different. Curious and alive to everything, he'd patiently and generously shown her how to listen to music, and it took both, she recognised, to get to her. Having come back to him in a humbled mood she agreed to leave when he suggested it and once outside took his arm gratefully, but there was resistance.

"Why were you so rude to Paul " he asked instantly.

"Me rude to him?"

"Don't you see what a position it puts me in? "

"Why? - it was my rudeness!" She looked disappointed.

"He was pleasant - even flirtatious - with you. He likes teasing you, that's all. You behave as if he's being spiteful."

"Secretly he is, but it's done in a way that looks okay. I like his knowing I positively dislike him."

130

"It puts you in the wrong. Makes you uncouth and eccentric."

"Good." Her face flushed and her eyes filled with tears. "You mustn't cart me around as an embarrassment," she said quietly.

3

A few days later Winifred arranged a visit with a friend in Scotland who for months had been trying to persuade her to come and see her. Instead of its seeming too big a break in her work pattern it now felt like the only place left she could work.

Barbara had married as soon as she left Cambridge and the friendship had continued by post. Her husband was a sort of peripatetic education officer for the Western Highlands. Already she had two children. They lived in a stone cottage at Locharron where Robert had recently installed electricity - she'd been celebrating the fact for pages in her last letter. He spent a great deal of time away from home, leaving her hungry for company and she was overjoyed at Win's sudden suggestion.

She greeted her on the doorstep with open arms. They were still hugging when a highpitched scream behind them scared Win into breaking free. Wailing followed.

"It's only Sam being Sam," Barbara said, taking Win's bag and meeting a tearstained toddler in the hallway. He stuck his thumb in his mouth and clutched her skirt, hobbling her progress to the sittingroom and eyeing Win nervously over his shoulder. Barbara sat, picked him up and turned him to face her on her lap. He plopped out his thumb.

"Got it! Sam got it!" he said. Barbara saw the dirty white rabbit he was clutching in his other hand.

"Give it back, you little devil!"

Her temper was so instant Win felt she'd interrupted an ongoing battle and at that moment became conscious of a startling smell she couldn't define. Barbara got up again carrying Sam to the back of the house where she gave the rabbit to the pinkfaced source of the wailing sitting up in a pram. Coming back through the kitchen Win saw nappies boiling on the stove and couldn't help saying, "Wouldn't paper ones be better? "

She was ignored. The reality suddenly hit her like a brick. She'd committed herself for a fortnight to an exclusive, powerful and foreign world. The dynamics she always seemed to be looking for had in this case nothing to do with her but refused her a simple watching role. She was assaulted, taken by storm and left. Barbara saw her face and grinned, indicating with a wave of her hand toys, nappies, linen basket, baby's pot, loose pages of a magazine and one free hardbacked chair.

"How are you, Win? " she said, almost with concern.

"Fine." Win was still standing.

"Let's shove these bits on the table and you can sit here." Joan lifted a pile of dry nappies from a softer chair and Winifred sat down. Barbara, head on one side, smiled sympathetically. "Bit of a shock, eh? "

Win nodded. The toddler had followed his mother holding on to her apron and was now staring at Winifred with dauntless curiosity. She smiled timidly. He gave no sign of having seen it. She felt more and more uneasy.

"You look tired," her friend said, "and I think thinner than ever."

"I'm okay. Bit tired from travelling."

"What a fool I am! I'll get you some coffee. Have you eaten? "

"Coffee would be lovely."

She went out to put on the kettle and, abnormally stimulated, knocked Sam over. He picked himself up chasing unsteadily after her, fist outstretched half in protest half in appeal.

Winifred sighed as soon as she was alone. Barbara had changed. The careless clumsy confidence was new, so was the plumpness.

In a moment she was back, Sam in her arms and no coffee. She stood holding him, turning him outwards towards Win.

"Lovely boy," Win said, "beautiful eyes."

"Yes!" - instantly confidential and relaxed - "it's an evil little nature though" - tickling him in the region of his plump tummy. He caved in around it in silent laughter and turned a full and serious gaze on Winifred.

She felt her response now would be crucial, got up and put her hand to his cheek. "Hallo, Sam." Her voice was warm but nervous and he ducked, turning to his mother, lower lip trembling. Barbara rocked him.

"He's not used to strangers - doesn't see many people."

Winifred nodded.

"He has a little sleep in a few minutes. Then we can have a chat."

About an hour later when Sam was asleep, the baby fed and put down and Winifred unpacked they had the promised chat. It was about Sam, how he had reacted to the birth of Clare the eight-month-old, and how his resentment was slowly turning into protectivity - Barbara illustrating maturity with a few cherished examples. Winifred listened and felt more alone than at Cambridge. They'd had so much in common when they were undergraduates. She sat quietly now answering in monosyllables.

Barbara saw she was stressed. Poor girl - a spinster, beginning to look every inch of it, and she used to be so full of life! She'd imagined such long and interesting talks and there she sat, tight and negative.

"That's enough of my boring domestic problems," she said at last, "how are things with you? Working hard?"

"Not really. Research gets you down," and Win briefly outlined the thesis so far.

"To think I seriously wanted to do it myself at one time! - thank God I didn't get a First!"

"You live in a beautiful place, Barbara" - Win changed the subject to something they could share - "tell me some good walks close by."

Things weren't as bad as Winifred had feared. Reminiscences of Cambridge in the next few days helped loosen things up but what really stood them in good stead was a mutual and growing curiosity. Neither could believe the other had changed so much. They were hunting out what they felt must still be there and the next few days helped them find it. The startled look mixed with pleasure in Win's eyes when she was handed the baby and the flash of anger in Barbara's when Sam snatched off a playing record helped them see they'd been sulking over disappointed memory. This was live and new - the person they remembered had simply adapted to something different.

The understanding was slow. At first Winifred was furious at the family's tyranny over Barbara and fiercely resisted the assumption that she was more grist for the mill. She thought Barbara obsessive over her duties and deaf to anything with less impact than a scream but found the circumstances having a similar effect on herself. She'd capture the struggling toddler and go through a wild performance of laughing and tickling to win him over to do what he didn't want to. Sometimes it worked and when she saw she could have some effect she was flattered and tried harder.

From that point she was a real help to Barbara, who was warmer and grateful. Every thought, every interest not intimately connected with the apparently haphazard but in fact inflexible routine of the household was nipped in the bud, and by being on loan to it Win discovered the odd moments when Ba was receptive to other things and would surface with a bright look at something said. She was curious about Win's relationship with John and her dissatisfaction with her work but as she was beginning to share her world her husband came back from a longish tour of duty.

Win knew very little about Robert and was interested. She tried to goad him into saying something on his first evening back but he wouldn't have it - he was tired, glad to be home and disappointed at having his normal routine spoilt by a stranger. He chatted only enough to make it clear he didn't really resent her presence.

Later in the week Win saw the domestic picture in another light. They were sitting in front of a coal fire one evening - Robert's legs pointed towards the centre of comfort, blocking the other two from moving closer. Win was sitting with her book closed hoping someone would say something. Barbara was knitting. Robert's thin face ruddy in the firelight showed a faint uneasiness as if he'd begun to feel some pressure to open his mouth coming from Win's general direction.

"What are you reading? " he asked.

"*Middlemarch* again. Right now I can't find anything I like so much."

"Nice! I didn't know we had it." He yawned; his eyelids were swollen.

"We don't, she brought it with her!" Barbara didn't look up as she said it.

"Didn't think you'd find it on our shelves," he said in the middle of another yawn, "we've burnt our books, haven't we, darling?"

No answer.

"Got rid of 'em to make more room for kids. Did you know she wanted more? " Win looked interested. "Two in three years isn't enough, we need four in six."

Barbara yawned. Win wondered if they'd fall asleep, and panicked. "Really, Ba? You really want more kids? "

"Mmm," nodding rhthmically.

"But she still moans about never doing anything interesting," Robert said.

"I don't!"

"Well, you've been kidding me then. I've always suspected you like being half asleep all the time."

"Fat chance!"

"Too tired to read or talk, she tells me."

"Why bother, you're off before I am."

"Even too tired to read the cookbook I bought her!"

Win decided it might be better if they did fall asleep.

"I've given her a chance to go sloppy," he told her in mock confidence. "She's a real drag in the evenings nodding off over knitting or whining for television."

"If you'd get a telly I wouldn't nod off!"

136

"I'd rather you nod off." The amused smile he gave Win didn't work and he rallied again to meet the challenge of a third person. "I must say" - his eyes brightened - "it's refreshing to see a lively woman - could you help her remember she was one once?"

Win, grinning nervously, picked up her book, and seeing he'd made yet another mistake he abandoned the attempt to entertain. Getting up he stretched and went over to squeeze Barbara's shoulder and ask her if she'd like some coffee.

"You do mean now, don't you? " she asked.

"Well, I thought I'd write some reports first."

"I thought so. I'll bring something in later." He closed the door. "He's not serious, you know," she said immediately trying to wipe out the tension in Win's face. "Really he's chalking up his success. Thinks he's no end clever converting me from bluestocking to housewife."

Win looked puzzled. "Do miss your own life?"

"Not at the moment."

"Doesn't he want anything more?"

"Seems to like what he's got." She put down her knitting and yawned. "For the time being, I suspect - same with me." There was a pause. "You can see for yourself he's no livelier - but that'll change as the children grow up." She yawned again. "I'll cross that bridge when I come to it."

"And you want more children?"

"Why not?"

"Puts off the evil hour?"

Ba's face grew serious. "If you marry, won't you want children?"

"Haven't thought along those lines yet - guess I'll come to it. How is it, changing your whole way of life?" Win asked suddenly.

137

"How is it?" A pause. "I suppose it sneaks up on you. If you want something I suppose you're ready to lose something in the process. Sam's birth frightened me - the pain took me by surprise - you can't educate yourself to it -but bodies have short memories. I remember feeling the pain and urgency was all there was. Once it was gone - and it wasn't something you overcame by an effort of will, it just suddenly stopped with the appearance of the baby - I felt incredibly grateful. To be let off the hook probably but it transferred to the child. A long while afterwards I realised I'd forgotten what it was like to be a single self."

That excited Winifred.

"It knocked all the spoilt brat out of me. We're lucky to be women. Men don't seem to get there. What a relief to know life's got nothing to do with notions."

The following morning Win was taking a different interest in the household events. She stared at Barbara a lot, watched her tired face (the baby got her up every night) irritably scolding her son or abjectly making up to him for an undeserved clout, and tried to bring it in line with what she'd said. In spite of herself she was feeling sad and out of it again. She seemed to lose the knack she had with Sam. The children upset her. Offered the baby girl to hold she shook her head. A confident autocracy in the baby's yelling angered and moved her. Sam, more sure of himself with her, sometimes took pains to endear himself. She enjoyed that but it was a double-edged pleasure. It would have been wholly good if she'd been accepted as a substitute for Ba but for anything serious she found she didn't exist. He'd give his attention or affection when things were going well but they were pretty rare occasions for him since the baby was born.

Win fell back on her work. It seemed amazing she hadn't

got down to it before. Here she'd really get things done - if only she got out of the way. She got out of the way but nothing happened.

It left only one thing to do, walking. This was a success. Removing herself at one level and coming back at another was what work had always done for her and now she achieved the same effect in walking, relishing the dark cold lakes and mountain roads with lonely intensity. It was where the missing passion lay. The alchemy of mountain air and scenery converted instantly to a passion for life and she trembled at the sudden appearance of four new mountain peaks as she got to the top of a long climb. White creviced rock gleamed like snow in the sunlight.

4

Winifred went back to Cambridge determined to make her relationship with John work and for a while it seemed to. She buried discontent and a sense of imbalance in gratitude and hoped the holiday they'd finally planned to take together would be a turningpoint.

On the appointed day in June, waiting for their train on a crowded platform, they looked through a heat haze at a dancing track reverberating with their own excitement. Win found herself moving among the holidaymakers with ease and flexibility at last. Excitement transformed her. She belonged. Gleaming-faced, confident she watched John fetch some tea from the buffet and smile at a girl standing by. She saw him roused by her bare neck and arms - it wasn't a betrayal but an overflow. His nervous self-control drove her wild and as he came back she was trembling.

On the train to Cornwall their concentration on each other was broken up and Winifred was amazed at John's finding the peace of mind to read. Disappointed one way, reassured another, she slumped back in her seat. From now on it was all waiting.

They arrived at seven o'clock exhausted. He'd rallied a little and under his efficiency was a quiet, delicate solicitousness she mistrusted. She couldn't get back her morning confidence.

The town stretched along a cliff edge giving them glimpses of the sea between hotels, and when they couldn't resist any longer they took a path towards it. An immense heaving expanse of ocean was breaking into cold waves below them.

"Have you ever seen anything like it?" John asked.

She had her hands to her ears against the buffeting and didn't hear.

"Glad we came?" he shouted. His shirt was billowing to one side, his open jacket cracked in the wind like a flag. She nodded. Looking at her excited face he stood close, not seeming to want to touch her but share what she was feeling.

She grew more and more afraid of what felt like his impersonality. There were no assurances - how could there be, with him or anyone else? The wind caught her off balance once or twice and the world, darkening and growing cold, was beginning to feel unsound. They were passing a deserted cliff shelter when John pulled her into it. Overhot and glistening, his embrace was too hard and she pictured herself breaking away, while her body accepted his hold as unbreakable.

On the bus that took them the last lap of their journey Winifred fell deeply asleep. She was unloaded twenty minutes later, blinking, trying to collect herself and finding she was in a new place full of trees. She looked confused.

"You shouldn't have fallen asleep," he said, taking her case and looking up the hill ahead of them. "The guesthouse is up there, you'll be alright in a minute." She tried to keep hold of his sleeve but he gently shook her off. Grabbing it back she looked at him with exposed, unsettled eyes that were unsettling him and beginning to make him irritable. He got free under the pretext of changing the cases round.

A short way up there was a bridge over a rushing stream and Win rested on it watching a boy engrossed in selecting pebbles. His bare legs stuck out like stripped twigs, jerking backwards and forwards from stone to stone, splitting the water. She could just make out his face.

If the idea of living with John was threatening, the idea of a child wasn't. The memory of Barbara made her see that this decision on a single week with no further commitment was a mistake. The only thing they'd have would be sex - it put too strong a focus on something that might take years to get right. Marriage should be like choosing a job. How far you got depended on how much you put into it. And this whole scheme was hers! She was the one needing constant reassurance - and this week was supposed to provide it? She'd trapped herself in lies - and suddenly she started crying.

John thought he'd grown used to the frequency of her mood changes but the occasions for them never stopped surprising him. "What's the matter now? I'll wish we hadn't come if you go on like this."

"Don't say that! We'll have a wonderful week!"

"What are you crying for, then?"

"I don't know."

The guesthouse turned out to be small. Two middle-aged sisters owned and ran the place - businesslike, curious and on their own terms communicative. It put more strain on Win - she needed anonoymity to deal with what was already too much.

As she'd expected, sex made more problems than it solved - they both needed a reassurance they daren't ask for.

On the third morning at breakfast they were all (there were two other couples) looking out on a rainsoaked garden. One pair looked depressed, assessing their chances of getting out at all, the other talked about getting a taxi to the nearest town. Win and John seemed not to mind. Her face was almost vacant of expression but his grey eyes had a fugitive brightness. They ate without talking.

Afterwards John bustled her into her raincoat but her first spontaneous act was to make a dash for the road when she saw the younger sister was coming over to apologise for it all. What was wrong with her? Why couldn't she chat for a second?

Safely out, John told her they were walking to the sea which was about two miles away. She enjoyed holding his wet hand and having warm rain trickle off her chin but soon the wet warmth and close dungy smell of the fields began to excite the sexuality that hadn't been satisfied. John bent a forefinger to his lips to stifle a yawn and freed she walked ahead at a smart pace - a sense of power and freedom growing with every step.

She stopped suddenly to stand on the bottom rail of a gate for a view across the fields. Too much rain! A corner was interesting - deeply rutted and muddy. The whole field smelt of pigs. She got up higher, leaning over to peer round. There was an enormous hog pushing his nose in the mud again and again - rain streamed off his back, emphasizing power and intensity. The vicious biting smell became strong enough to break her concentration - then she heard John. She watched him wrinkle his nose and inspect his shoes.

"Pigs," she said.

"Ah, splendid farmyard smell!" - pulling her down - "this is the life!" - and she nodded without looking at him.

"You and I were closer last night," he said after a bit. She blushed, half angry. He wiped some drips off his nose and pushed back his hair, giving her a chance to break away and she was off again.

Angry with herself and him she turned to wait for him and saw him standing in the middle of the road staring at a patch of oil. She rushed back, threw her arms round him and moved her hands to the cheeks of his bottom, fondling, her fingers tightening.

It took her the rest of the day to forget it but in the evening, after swimming and walking, it felt as if she had. They were looking out of their bedroom window listening to a wren and he had his arm round her.

"I wondered where she was, look darling, there she is!" He was pointing to a small compact body in the tree just outside, so concealed by leaves she could hardly see it.

She heard it more clearly now - rising streams of sound in endless, exhausting spiritual outpouring - and dragged herself away to sit on the bed.

"Isn't it incredible!" he said, coming to put his arms round her again. "A tireless fountain of sound from a body that size." Win's face was pale and obstinate. "As a physical presence she's hardly there," he went on, "but what a song!"

"Hardly there?" Anger rising, she checked it instantly but wasn't quite able to stop and finished ominously: "She's about her business!"

They made it up later in bed and the rest of the week she seemed quiet and loving. John set about proving not only his love but his willingness to do and be whatever she wanted. He was intense, solicitous and asked pardon for very little, until Win loathed herself beyond endurance for having made it happen.

On the last day they took the pig walk to the sea and a sudden pelting of warm rain roused old memories.

"How marvellous things are now!" he said happily.

They turned into a lane and Winifred broke into easy natural smiles for the first time. The light was brightening and she broke into a run - hard wet road, thick grass, quick clouds and she was over the top with excitement. When John caught her up she looked radiant.

"What was that about?" he asked happily.

"Can't wait for a swim!"

She changed in the shadow of a rock and rushed into the water with the manic ungainliness of a stranded fish escaping to its element.

5

In the kitchen Mrs Whittam felt and behaved as if she were at war. The passive immoveable presence of so much grease-smeared formica and stainless steel was converted in her mind to an active insult - like a smack in the face each morning - and she reacted accordingly. It was battle to the death and at 48 she was beginning to feel exhausted by it. Occasionally a spark of the old spirit, at this moment projecting a dishcloth up the side of the wall before it fell into place, came back unbidden but mostly she just looked angry when she entered the room. She took the tea tray she'd been preparing to the sittingroom and put it down next to the stereo where John's music was playing relentlessly loud and penetrating.

The room was like a shoebox with the ends cut off. Large windows at either end destroyed privacy and at the road-facing windows she kept the curtains permanently drawn, hardly ever seeing the untidy couple of yards of grass outside. Her house was one of dozens of others like it, the others kept anonymously clean and tidy, hers having the distinction of failing to do either. She thought the other inhabitants were probably secretly in touch with each other but she knew nothing about their lives. It angered her. She felt exposed to judgments based on notions she wanted nothing to do with.

The music was becoming impossible - fighting for the attention she couldn't give because she wanted to talk. She couldn't tell John to turn it down for fear of putting restraints on him that would make him shorten his stay, and stood beaten about the head with sound. It was made worse by the gnawing anticipation of an explosion of sharp knocks on the wall from the woman next door. Mrs Whittam was only semi-detached and regarded her neighbour with contemptuous dread.

She handed a cup of tea to John who was spreadeagled in a deep armchair - arms flung over its arms suspended level with his shoulders, it took him seconds to get into the right position for taking it. There was a good relationship between them based largely on the fact that she was a moral warrior who couldn't find a justifiable way of giving herself his human rights. She made few demands on him, restraining herself when her natural intensity suggested the opposite. At those times she battled out her conflicting feelings alone and usually all John saw was an increased pallor in her normally thin and unhealthy face. She enjoyed fighting herself and winning. It gave her something to live for - even made her in a way self-sufficient - but the renewed pleasure of winning had an acid taste by comparison with the sweet unsolicited trust and affection her son gave in return - when he was around.

"What time you on at the library?" he asked between sips.

"Don't think I'll go, John." She was hesitant, waiting for signs of agreement. "It's only your second day home - I haven't had a chance to talk to you yet. I can say my cold got worse."

"Don't do that - you hate facing out lies."

Obviously he didn't want to talk and she nodded agreement: "We'll talk when you're ready."

"Nothing to tell. No major surprises in finals!"

"I wasn't thinking of them. You haven't said anything about your holiday."

He reached for a biscuit and listened to the final bars of the sixth Brandenburg. When it stopped the room seemed desolate and his energy had gone with it but he had to say something:

"Win said she'd come back with me for a couple of days but had to go to her foster parents instead. Their daughter's getting married."

"Oh." Undoubtedly the facts, she thought, but it didn't feel like the truth. Every signal she'd picked up from him had other reverberations - undertones of exhaustion and anxiety and traces of misery that seemed to have no cause. "I'd like to see her - she sounds interesting."

"She'll come some other time," he said hesitantly, "she's a strange woman."

"Might you marry her?"

"I'd like to."

"And her? "

"I think so."

She smiled as if satisfied, took the cup off the arm of his chair and went back to the kitchen to make sandwiches for work.

"How many weeks before you get your results?" she shouted.

"Four or five."

"You'll be looking round before then?"

"Suppose so, hadn't thought about it."

"Any ideas about what you'd like to do?"

He got up slowly and went to her so they wouldn't have to shout. "Only what I wouldn't. Teaching's out. An office feels like prison - but what about the library?" he said, perching his head on her shoulder from behind. She knew it was a joke. "Or an obscure post in a publisher's office?"

"Better start making some serious enquiries," she said gently, "if that's what you'd like. They won't expect you to wait for your results."

"I need a rest."

She washed up the cups in a hushed fashion, and feeling her thinking behind the dishcloth he went back to put on another record.

Three or four days went by without John's hearing from Winifred. They'd separated at Exeter and John had gone straight on to Birmingham. In these few days he rested and dreamed, mostly unhappily. He adored Winifred but felt so insecure about her there was almost a sense of loss. Her gentleness with him at the end of the holiday had intensified his love - he'd thought it evidence of final acceptance but couldn't quite react as if it were. He'd never fully understood her but trusted her. For all her intensity she was gentle.

His main concern was overcoming the boredom and denial of the next three weeks until he met her again at Sylvia's wedding. He wished he'd made more effort to see her sooner but her request seemed reasonable. She had to concentrate on the wedding and her foster parents. John admired the strength of her sense of duty. It reminded him a little of his mother's. She was passionate yet somehow selfless and spiritual, and the sadness he was feeling was the product of his own selfish nature. His punishment was that he was the one who always felt life was difficult. She seemed to have no sense of it. One of the joys of Win's nature was that she never seemed to get depressed - angry but not depressed. She expected, insisted life be good - and in general it seemed that for her it was. Things were more lively around her. He'd be happy with her.

He read, listened to records and went for long walks in the Warwickshire countryside to pass the time but avoided talking to his mother and as the days wore on and there was still no letter he became more tight-lipped than ever. He wondered if Win were ill and consoled himself with the thought that the family would let him know if she were. He wrote every day as he'd promised. She'd seemed to like the idea at the time. She must be up to her ears in wedding hassle to have no time to answer. Not a bad omen, perhaps.

6

"I'd say she needs a dose of her own medecine," Paul said, bending towards his fork while John was staring at his plate. They were eating at the Trojan again. John, unable to wait at home any longer, had taken up Paul's offer to stay with him if he was at a loose end. Almost as soon as they'd met he'd blurted out his anxiety.

"She's not a bitch, Paul. Something must have gone wrong. Perhaps Sylvia got cold feet and Win's trying to sort things out."

"She'll be popular!"

"Anyway, I've decided if I don't hear by the end of the week I'm going down."

"Don't chase after her, for Christ's sake!" Paul set his jaw and John felt dashed - even so he wouldn't settle for Paul's view of it.

"You don't know what it's like. Wait till you find the woman you want to live with. There's no room for role-playing. Win would be hurt if I didn't go and find out."

"Don't do it, John. If you want to make it permanent there's no room for anything else. Play it cool, she'll come running."

John shrugged. "It's not like that."

"Everything's like that! Tell you what, I'll introduce you to somebody new at the party tonight. Don't have to be serious - last thing you need. Toy with the idea." Paul was a 'party' man - if he had a problem he held a party.

John turned up. At first it was an endurance test. He

leaned his long thin body up a bookcase waiting to feel the urge to join in. Where was the promised fun? Noisy, affected, pretending to have a good time - they made him feel worse. With a little more drink he looked a little closer. There were lots of girls. Ever since he'd known Winifred he'd given up eye-games and now, looking round, found the urge coming back. Part of him must have wanted to come here - he'd taken the trouble to dress up. There was an inaccessibility of spirit in his face that he was sure piqued or challenged many women. He liked that. He could have a good time and keep his distance while they did all the work. He had a fine mouth. Win had told him it suggested a subtler sensuality than Paul's big one.

The wine was working overtime. His affectionate self-appraisal made him look for corroboration, which he found in at least one pair of eyes. Bending to put his glass on the table, he looked up suddenly at the girl who'd been watching him hardest. Her eyes flared.

To Milly Brettle that easy looseness of body spoke experience and the glance energy.

His hand lingered round the glass, overdoing it a little, and he glanced to see if he'd spoilt things. Not a bit. She was holding a bantering conversation with two men while giving him her unbroken attention. He smiled briefly and looked for Paul.

Paul was resting his hand on a blonde's shoulder but his head was turned away as if her breath smelt. He was working out his next move, John thought. The sight filled him with self-disgust and for a moment he thought of leaving. He tried imagining what it would be like if Winifred were with him. She'd talk, ask questions - they'd be transformed from grimacing predators to uncertain people hoping for a good time.

He found he'd become jammed between two backs and was facing the excited eyes from a fresh angle. A friendly squeeze on the arm turned him to Paul who was pushing him gently towards her. Why not?

"This is Mill, John - Milly Brettle, just finished at Homerton. Going to teach infants in September, aren't you, love?" He put his hand on her cheek. "I'll leave you two to get acquainted. I'm going back to attend to my June flower or she'll be sitting on someone else's lap." He grinned and moved off.

Milly and John smiled at each other. The next step was more difficult but he'd noticed her glass was empty which gave him a chance - "Like some more?" - amazed at the intimacy in his tone.

"It's all red and rough - or do you know where there's something better?" She was smiling and blushing as if the comment had other meanings.

Adjusting to the speed things were happening he took his time fetching it. She was so roused when he came back he headed her off, alarmed.

"Where you going to teach now you're qualified?"

"Here. Just outside, really - Betterton village school." She knew he wanted her to go on talking. "I'd rather teach country kids till I get the hang of it - then I'm heading back."

"Where?"

"London - can't you tell? I thought I still sounded Cockney. Country kids are easier to handle." Her words were coming too fast, she blushed.

"Got a place to live?"

"Yes, sharing a flat with a friend who's still got a year to go - then back home, I hope."

He shifted closer. About time! Someone moved into the gap and she found his arm pressed against hers. It took her entire concentration to carry on talking, the words now making a high-pitched monotone:

"I've been going steady with a chap doing Maths at Emmanuel" - why was she telling him this? - "but it's fallen through. As long as I was ready for bed when he was it was fine - mention settling down and family and you saw his Hyde side! Silly to imagine he'd change but I did. Seemed a domestic sort underneath. We had a row...." She looked up, blinded by the present.

How charmingly she laid her cards on the table - his eyes were showing sly appreciation and he touched her fingers in taking her glass. On the way to the bottle he tripped over a foot and the wine rushed to his head - on the way back he leaned on someone's shoulder and they laughed - how friendly and close everyone was!

He gave her the drink and put his arm round her waist, drawing her to the corner of the room where a couple had got out of an armchair. He flopped in, pulling her on top. Relief at not having to pretend any more made her fling her arms round him.

7

Next morning Milly gave a blow-by-blow account of the previous evening to her flatmate Marion. Marion was making coffee. They were in a small ill-decorated kitchen where an oldfashioned cooker took all of one wall. Marion was bored. She shifted cups, banged tins and sniffed coffee. Milly went back to the sittingroom but her voice was still at it:

"I couldn't believe it - I didn't expect him to be more than chatty. I still can't believe it. I've been kissed before but never like that!" Marion rolled her eyes. "It wasn't the drink - I've had more than that before. He came on so strong." She was looking out of the window. "But he isn't the sort to go to parties for that - before me, he'd just been standing about looking miserable." She looked into the street and her voice went lower. "He's got a girlfriend, Paul says." And after a long pause, "What shall I do? "

"I don't know."

"Why, aren't you listening?" She took her coffee. "Ought I be out when he comes today? I'm not going to be jilted again."

"Ask him," Marion said sitting.

"Ask him what? "

"If it's serious with the other girl."

Milly was cross. "I can't sit at our first lunch and ask if he's serious about someone else."

"Why not? "

Milly turned away in disgust.

"That or something like it." Marion didn't want a row and her tone was semi-apologetic.

"Would *you* after one meeting? I'm not even supposed to know he's got a girl."

"What then? "

"I'll wait and see if he tells me."

"That's the ticket!" Marion had a regular boyfriend, she'd left all this behind.

The coffee warmed Milly to a rosier frame of mind and going to the window again she imagined John walking down the street and coming for her in a couple of hours. She glanced at the clock - time for a bath.

Soaking and dreaming she went into a steamy trance

reliving last night's excitement. It came back so strong she was exhausted when she came out - so tired in fact her feelings were changing again and she was ready to believe it would be another failure. She'd never find an easy, loving man she could admire and would let her live the life she wanted. Perhaps she was looking in the wrong places. Her daydream paled in front of the men she took up with.

Spreading the wet towel over the back of a chair, a consolatory dream took over. She was picking up a little girl who'd fallen and hurt herself, smoothing the strands of hair from her face, making her smile. Her dreams were so vivid real life was purgatory afterwards.

When John called at lunchtime she was overjoyed to see a look of surprise - admiration even - in Marion's face. A splitsecond change in her eternally casual manner was the most reassuring thing that could have happened.

They caught a bus with other Sunday couples - Milly glowing with pride when he had to stoop before sitting. Her burning sense of conquest made it impossible to take her eyes off his long legs. Looking round she saw no-one who matched him and her stomach tightening with glee, her movements quick and light, she stared up at the conductor with an open, curious gaze that won him instantly - the world was hers!

John had never felt so confident with a woman. The perfect impression seemed to have been made and with no effort on his part - he was free to be himself. So this was what it should be like. One in the eye for Win! The potential treachery to both women was fast becoming one of the most exciting things he'd ever done. They had their fish to fry. He had his. For the first time he found himself facing up to the misery and resentment he'd been feeling over the last few weeks.

At lunch they had a good time saying little and relishing their separate prospects and when the time came they got up as one to go for the walk in the woods he'd suggested.

Outside in the fresh air her heart raced, taking his arm was enough. This was it - sex but more than sex. A sudden panic at being carried away made her withdraw her arm. If he let her down!

Tree trunks, a heady air of green leaves thickening, slowing and intoxicating them, left no choice but at the first sheltered place to make love - and afterwards he was begging for more:

"Come to my place tonight, I'll get Paul to go out."

She nodded, swinging into his arms again, and behind it the gleam of permanence was turning the experience into a semi-religious one.

He was impressed at her naturalness and confidence. She abandoned herself completely - played no manipulative games. He was amazed how refreshed he felt.

8

Back in her room the prospect of spending the night with him seemed dangerous. She'd told him she needed to collect some things but what she'd thought would be a resting space was filled with anxiety.

Marion had been washing her hair and was in front of the mirror rolling it on curlers. On a chair by her side was a pile of them with lotions, pins, combs and brushes. Milly looked on with envy. Self-preparation was good for morale if nothing depended on it.

It was Marion who eventually broke the silence and asked how she'd got on. The question was casual but if she asked at all she was interested. The memory of her glance earlier gave Milly the confidence she needed.

"I think I'm in love," she said suddenly.

Marion waited. She was tempted to remind her of her other 'love' but decided against it. She found herself wanting to know more about this one but a cynical scepticism wouldn't quite move over.

"More than Richard?" she asked.

Milly didn't answer.

"The other girl's no problem?" she tried once more. Glancing in the mirror she saw Milly smiling. It alarmed her. John was a catch. She herself was fixed up but had dreams of doing better - dreams the girls had shared when Milly was going steady before.

"Seeing him again soon?"

"Spending the night - Paul's going out - I came back to collect some things" - then suddenly in a defenceless tone she asked, "Am I being a fool?"

Something in it made Marion feel Milly wasn't talking strategy and it made her more uneasy. The game, the glamour, the strategy were the reality they'd accepted. Half narcissistic, half erotic fantasy dressed any dish to satisfy a basic need but this felt different - as if the experience were more rivetting than the objective.

"Be careful, remember last time."

"Last time was different. I slipped in by degrees. I wanted to and didn't want to for so long that in the end there wasn't any point in not doing it. Anyway I wanted to find out about sex - see if it was all it was cracked up to be."

Marion tried to drive her in the old direction: "How different though, apart from the speed?"

Milly was taking off her shoes and gave her an irritable sideways look. Shoe in hand she paused to make the right answer. "He's what I *really* want."

Marion's stomach turned over. "And the other girl?"

It was as if Milly hadn't heard - she was looking for something in a drawer.

"For instance, how would he take it if you put him off?"

"I shan't put him off."

This wasn't a lockout, it was new territory. Real exposure was dangerous, you dreamed about it only. Milly had gone into the bathroom and realising she might stay there till John arrived Marion shouted, "Milly!"

No answer.

"Milly, can you hear? "

"What? "

She got up and stood outside the door. "Do you care so much nothing else matters?" There was a long silence. Marion's voice had sounded so childlike Milly barely recognised it.

"Yes," she answered after a pause.

"What if he leaves you? "

After a longer pause Milly replied, "He won't," in a confident voice.

"Why not? "

"He's not the type. Too sensitive to others - principled too. I don't mean he's soft, I just get the feeling it would be misery to him to let someone down."

"Aah!" The relief in Marion's voice was so clear Milly thought she must care for her more than she'd suspected and went on to put her more at ease:

"He's sort of oldfashioned."

Marion went happily back to her curlers. "I'll make you a cup of tea in a minute," she shouted.

Milly came out shortly afterwards with a plastic holdall and towel and dumped them on the bed. "I've butterflies in my stomach."

"Drown 'em," Marion said going out to make the drinks. When she came back she saw Milly had put her hair up and it gave her plump face an exposed and slightly stupid look. She smiled.

Wandering aimlessly cup in hand Milly told herself she'd come back to think things out and hadn't done it yet. After all what did it matter? - she wouldn't be any worse off than before. It would be wonderful though if everything worked out - better than anything she'd imagined.

When John did arrive Marion was more than ever enheartened at the fact that he noticed her. Preoccupied in a predatory way with getting Milly away he still gave her appreciative glances. The three of them huddled in the doorway a moment before the two went off.

9

John felt so carefree the following morning that after seeing Milly back and arranging a meeting for the same evening he found himself looking for the best way to enjoy his freedom. First he phoned his mother to say he'd probably be staying the week. She was unusually talkative, full of bits and pieces of information and coming to the main point only after several minutes. Merther's the publishers had offered him an interview for the following Monday at 10.30. He told her he'd be back on Sunday and calmed her anxiety at opening his letter. Just the same she went on justifying herself and labouring for the understanding he'd already given. It was a way of expressing some of her feelings while giving him room to smile at them and he left the phone box feeling there wasn't a relationship in the world he couldn't handle.

He didn't think much about Winifred and when he did it was no longer anxiously. He'd established a balance. Some time in the future he'd tell her about Milly and she'd see what her insensitivity had been responsible for - he enjoyed the prospect.

The day was a marvel of freshness - a sky full of light and the street full of lively faces. For something to do he found himself catching a bus to Betterton and watching women's faces through the window and when he got there strolled through the village thinking of Milly. She'd helped him see the week with Winifred had been a failure, sexually at least. They'd both been too nervous and too conscious of each other. He even wondered if Win was afraid of writing till she'd thought it through. Perhaps she couldn't write as if everything were alright so couldn't start.

Apparently aimless walking brought him to the village school - lowbuilt, redbricked and quiet with its glistening playground stretching towards him in the sunlight. He leant on the warm wall and looked at battered swings with their seats tied round their poles. Near him a sagging-barred wooden climbing frame gave him sudden vivid impressions of buzzing energy indoors and shrieks in the playground. He loved children. Wherever they were he felt lightened, and Milly fitted the picture - relaxed and motherly, encouraging the curious and bossing the abstracted - full of unintense comfort, brief and effective. He was near to feeling he loved her when he realised that it was how he wanted to be himself - not what he needed in a mate. She couldn't help him live with himself or enhance the world for him.

At one time, before he met Winifred, he'd thought his lack of ambition a weakness, but found with her his sights had been set on other things. The memory of how well he seemed to explain himself to himself and how rich life was in her company gave him a sense of loss that stripped the scene of interest. With Win the world, good or bad, was live - the depressions and sense of insufficiency natural to him looked normal and as acceptable as any other responses to life - but he had to be with her all the time for it to work.

Envisaging a life with Milly felt like eternal misfittedness with comforts on the side. She'd expect what the rest of the world expected. Work would have to give him what she couldn't and he had no commitment to any form of it and no ambition.

On his walk back to town he grew more and more depressed with anxiety mounting at every step. At the flat he rushed upstairs bursting into Paul's room to leave a message and found Paul there looking surprised and pleased to see him.

"This is luck! I haven't had a chance to ask you...." He trailed off, seeing John red-faced and dazed.

"I was going to leave a note."

"What about?"

"Going to Exeter." He blurted it out like a schoolboy making confession and went redder.

At first Paul looked as if he didn't believe him, then for reasons John couldn't fathom looked angry - almost insulted. He went to his bedroom to let John get on with it.

On the journey to Exeter the thought persisted that in

spite of his mania he couldn't feel quite the same towards Winifred. She'd frightened him and forced him to make a fool of himself. He wasn't sure he could ever understand or forgive the long silence but at least their relationship would be clarified and he wouldn't have to go on like this. In the safety of the train he saw the trip had been prompted as much by the need to get away from Milly as to find Win.

He took a bus at Exeter to the suburb where Win lived and as he closed the space between started picturing the practicalities. He'd have her foster parents to deal with as well her. In embarrassing circumstances his strongest desires were capable of taking second place and at this moment it wasn't his strongest desire to face Win. Suppose his worst fears were true? Suppose she was using the wedding to fob him off?

He got off the bus where the driver told him and wandered around looking for the road. He was tired when he found it and checking numbers as he went hesitated at a blue gate that should have been 44. He peered up the path and saw a curtain move. He walked up it uneasily and rang the bell. A pleasant-faced woman with an enquiring smile opened the door.

"Mrs Nesbitt? "

"Yes."

"My name's John Whittam - you'll have heard of me."

She looked confused.

"Winifred's boyfriend."

"Of course," she said apologetically, "come in."

He'd made it this far and a moment later stood in the hall blinking and adjusting to the dull light. Mrs Nesbitt told him Win wasn't there and led him to her sittingroom. He was relieved as well as disappointed and sat in the offered chair.

When he looked up he saw she was flushed and tried to put her at her ease.

"I hope I haven't put you out - I'll only stay a moment - as soon as I've seen Win I'll go."

Her face had gone crimson then pale and her bright round eyes glanced from object to object in the room as if she were looking for something. "Yes, of course," she said, then looking suddenly out of the window she went over to rap sharply on it with her wedding ring. A few moments later Mr Nesbitt appeared in his socks, wiping his hands on his trousers.

John had been fully infected. He stood up, put out his hand and barely touching the other man's sat down again. From a sitting position and staring straight ahead he said, "I'm John Whittam - I've come to see Winifred."

Mr Nesbitt's face sagged. He took a furtive glance at his wife who was searching for anonymity among the furniture. "Didn't you get a letter?"

"No."

He studied John's knees. "She said she'd write - what a rotten trick!"

"She's not here then?" John asked in a highpitched voice.

"No. She's making some final visits in London." He didn't add anything and the silence went on for so long John had to speak:

"Has she gone with Sylvia?"

"Sylvia? Sylvia got married a couple of months ago and lives down the road." He looked at John's white face. "Have some tea and I'll explain what I can"- but even as he was talking John was moving to the door.

"Wait a bit," the older man said, "it was a shock to us all - I'd like to explain what I can."

John was frantic and understood only intermittently -
something about a man called Sidney.

"How long has she known him?" he asked.

"Who?"

"Sidney."

"It's not a man - it's in Australia."

This time he let him out of the door and down the
passage squeezing by him only just in time to open the
street door for him.

10

For days afterwards John wandered round his mother's
house as if he were homeless - bitterness and despair
locking him indoors till some violent eruption of anger
drove him out for long, draining walks. The anger was as
much against himself as Winifred. To have been so taken
in was a comment on his nature as well as his understanding. Part of him had wanted to be duped.

His mother, after the first panic, realised the illness
wasn't physical but his silence and remoteness made it
impossible to treat it any other way and she slipped into
habits and concerns from his post-pneumonia period, feeling mostly worried about his pallor and lack of interest in
food. Apathy towards treats she suggested and distractions
she put in his way became the thing to break through. Once
through the cure was in sight. She brooded about him at
the library and moved quietly about the house when she
came back and this was the the first external condition to
make its mark. It irritated him.

After a few days more he found himself putting on some music to break the stress of her silence. She took it as a promising sign. Questioning was still not on. She had to bite her tongue for fear he'd leave like a tomcat to brood it out somewhere else. One of her biggest trials was to suppress questions about the interview. He'd gone to it and come home with the same general air as when he'd left except for the addition of an unhealthy flush. She had to be content with, "I shan't get it - it was a deadly hole."

John was in fact beginning to notice stealthy movements of a more normal responsiveness. Half out of a need to protect it, half to keep going the healing side of his mother's anxiety a bit longer, he kept it to himself. The gloom and worry he was inflicting helped him handle his own - they were sharing his suffering. Eventually in a half-hearted way and mostly when alone he tried to read and to listen to the music he'd been only using before. He couldn't concentrate on the books, and the music he wanted to hear expected too much of him - the more it was a source of life the more it hurt.

The first event to jar him free was the letter from Winifred. Brief, distant but gentle, it simply explained that by the time he received it she'd be on her way to Australia. She'd written just before embarking, apologising for the pain it would give but confident he'd eventually be grateful he'd escaped an irritable partner. She said she'd always love his nature but couldn't live with it.

The note of sincerity was the most painful to deal with at this stage but her coolness helped him disengage. The anger he felt at her not being 'able to live with it' helped him place her in his mind. Such a cowardly decisiveness brought the first feelings of contempt for her he'd ever felt and when a few days later he got a letter from his college congratulating him on an Upper Second he was cured of her sufficiently to be pleased. His mother saw the spark and fanned it into a flame and for the first time John was deeply moved by her. After a few days more he found himself enjoying the evening out she'd insisted on to celebrate and over the meal talked about what he'd do now he was qualified - it wasn't the key he'd been looking for but would have to do. His three years at university had been justified.

He went to the city next morning looking for a gift for her - something fine yet intimate. He thought of a dress but couldn't face sorting through racks of them. He found the traffic and crowds exciting - the fact they were strangers even more so. He listened to snatches of conversation, noticed faces, expressions and gestures unrelated to his life but intimate with it. He took coffee in a cafe where a steamy atmosphere enclosed him like a fog, and felt soothed and rested. It was here he decided the gift should be a necklace from one of the antique shops he'd passed and in the afternoon he bought it - a medallion looking like a filigree sun hanging from a fine silver chain.

He prepared a meal that evening and when she came home she saw the table laid and him bending over it. She put her arms round him, breathing in delicious smells from the kitchen and he turned to pick her up in a delighted hug. They chatted through the meal as if they hadn't seen each other for months. She complained a little about the difficulties and boredom of her job, glad to let him into her life for a short time. She'd few friends, none of them intimate and the relief of just chatting as thoughts, complaints, even plans came into her head brought a flush of happiness. John capped her pleasure with his gift, pushing the parcel towards her over the table:

"I've got something for you."

165

She looked at him, brilliant-eyed, then down at the parcel, opening it with lingering fingers. As she took out the silver sun she checked her tears and the rush of love towards him, reminding herself that an expression of affection so intimate and unprompted might never be repeated now he was a man. She left her seat to stand behind his chair, kissing his hair and cheeks many times till John turned to take her hands and squeeze them. She couldn't recover her old control easily, tears wouldn't stop coming. The lines and texture of her face were softened and her eyes, searching for something in John's expression that would allow her to let herself go for a while and come to him for comfort, triggered the change she'd been expecting. He looked frightened. It seemed to him she might tell him of her loneliness and need for him, and kissing her hands he stood up.

The painful process of letting him go needed all the help it could get and she was almost grateful to him. A pity though that he couldn't trust her - but then she couldn't always trust herself.

11

The following day Mrs Whittam answered the phone and on an impulse covered the mouthpiece with her hand calling John in a loud whisper. He came in, wiping his hands on a teacloth.

"What?"

"A woman wants to talk to you - it's not just the publisher's."

He paused a moment. "Tell her I'm not in."

"I can't - I said you were."

"Give it me, then."

His mother handed over the phone, pushing it into his hands with a touch of alarm and annoyance.

"Hello," he said weakly, and she watched his expression change through deliberate vacuousness to discomfort and embarrassment. He turned towards her, covered the mouthpiece and wrinkling his face in an attempt to be casual asked if she'd mind dreadfully if he spoke to the woman alone.

She left the room instantly, shutting the door behind her. So, the fool was already involved with another woman! She'd no need to be told the affair with Winifred was over. She realised now she'd been anticipating a short period of intimacy with her son on the strength of it. And all the time he'd got another woman lined up. It was a pert, determined voice over the phone. Sounded confident. Coupling it with his embarrassment she decided he'd got himself into another mess. The idea of the girl's having a claim on him gave Mrs Whittam so much pain she stopped thinking about it and cleaned out the sink. At the end of it she saw clearly the folly of her panic. He'd have several girls now, the more the better. He was too young to be serious.

She heard the receiver click into place and waited for him to come out to her. He didn't. She went into the lounge and he was putting on an act with a paperback he'd just taken off a shelf.

"I've finished the washing up," she said.

"Sorry, I forgot."

She restrained herself from glancing at the title. "Who was that?"

"A girl I met at Paul's."

"Known her long?"

"About a fortnight."

His mother took down two library books from the same shelf. "Interested in her?"

He lifted his eyes for a moment. "Not going to be a jealous female after all this time, are you?"

She blushed. "Don't be absurd!" She picked up her bag from the floor and left the room. A few moments later he heard the street door close.

John had bought several newspapers that morning - he'd decided it was time to look for jobs in earnest. No use putting it off any longer - his good result changed the picture and now he was more nervous than reluctant, not getting a job was becoming the bigger threat. Happily, neither feeling was as disturbing as he'd thought it would be. Looking down the lists of vacancies he found a new ingredient had entered the game - he might go for money. Concerts, plays, trips abroad could keep him going - no point relying on anything else. Business might be the answer - he might even enjoy the power game. Was this what underpinned his friendship with Paul?

In spite of the exciting revelation of a new self he found himself reading and rereading an advert asking for 'a candidate with good Honours degree, Arts or Science, required to share in the teaching duties of King Arthur Preparatory School, Tintagel (attached to Somerson College for Boys). Previous teaching experience desirable but not essential.'

He still loved Cornwall. Obviously it was the location that caught his eye. Was he so well recovered from Win that the place was free of her? He'd always told himself he could stand any job if the place were beautiful enough to repair the damage. His mental picture of rough seas, wide skies, houses as part of the landscape or lost in sea-rain made such an appeal to the isolate in him that the prep school got lost in it, though on reflection it had its own appeal. Something had happened to the determination not to teach - it was beginning to look arbitrary. Training young children intensively in a sheltered environment felt attractive. The more he thought about it the better it felt. He liked the independence a job like this would give him. As a teacher he'd be left to his own devices and there'd be scope for his old commitments to life and art. The people he worked with would be 'like' souls - everything about it was beginning to feel right.

He applied for the post but also as a safety precaution to another publishing office and to the educational department of an Oxford bookshop. On rereading his letter to the school he felt he'd put himself over well and started waiting excitedly for an answer as soon as he'd posted it.

When his mother came home in the evening she found him chatty and goodhumoured.

"How d'you like the look of this?" he said passing over the paper when they were sitting together later. The advert was underlined.

"I thought you couldn't bear the thought of teaching."

"So did I!" He was laughing.

She raised her eyebrows.

"The countryside'll be good," he said, "and I'll be dealing with life, not just money, and I'll have some sort of independence." His mother was silent but he was looking hard at her, wanting support.

Staring into her lap she said, "I don't understand the change," then cheerily, "Well, I'm glad you're not going to be a librarian - lousy pay and deadly work. I sometimes think it's a calling for the weak-spirited."

"*You're* not that!" he said.

"Maybe."

"You could say it about any job," he added, glad to have her talking, "there are thousands of mouseholes - have to be, don't there? I'm not sure I'm not looking for one myself."

"Well, you won't find it there - not a peaceful one!" She pulled herself out of her chair and kissing him on the head went to bed.

12

There seemed to be no way of satisfying the restlessness his decision caused other than by changing his mind about Paul's recent letter. He decided to answer it. It wasn't as patronising as he'd thought on first reading. On second thoughts he could feel his way better by phoning. Paul was easy and relaxed and invited him to come right away if he felt like it.

The same morning Milly phoned again. There were a few tense and suspicious minutes that she deftly dispelled and he began to think she was an uncomplicated soul who took things at face value, and he rejoiced there was so little complaint or bullying in her. He told her he'd be in Cambridge for the next week.

On the journey he started reviewing the women and decided Winifred had somehow tricked him out of all the defences a sane man would put up. She'd lured him into devotion only to find she didn't like it. No danger of making the same mistake twice. The situation could be reversed with Milly. He'd walked out on her and she was acting as if it hadn't happened. If she were as affectionate and uncomplicated as she seemed it was just what he needed. He looked out of the train window at the dark-green August leaves. Generally he was oppressed by them - heat and lethargy had gone on too long and they carried the weight of it - but this time he didn't feel it. Locked in his own world, they were a backdrop to it. He was less exposed.

Milly made life seem easy. With her, as long as he kept up appearances he could go his own way, and this school job might give him the extra he needed.

John was pleased to see Paul's healthy face grinning at him in the doorway and Paul pleased to see his pale excited one.

"Good old John! I'm so glad you came," he said, clasping his hand.

Within ten minutes John felt he'd never left. They'd both done well in the exam, the future looked good and he was snatched into a bright world full of animal energy. Paul was going to work in his father's firm and was as excited as if it were a new world. John walked about the room expressing tentative optimism:

"We'll have good lives, I think"

"And it'll get better and better!"

John took the offered drink and settled down to it. "What are your plans?" Paul asked, and giving a sheepish smile John said:

"I think I'm going to teach."

Paul pretended to choke, "I thought you couldn't stand it - what does Winifred think?"

There was a brief silence. His reply - "It's got nothing to do with her" - took its time coming out.

Paul didn't question him and after a moment John told him the story.

"You mean she just whipped off without a word?"

"Yes."

Amazed and delighted, Paul was rubbing his hand against the side of his trousers, looking as if he'd won an argument without expecting to. He shifted about in his chair, grinning.

"Well, old pal, we can fill that gap."

John thought the revelation had gone off well and was grateful to Paul for his tact. There was a new sprightliness in Paul's movements as he strolled to the window, looked along the road and came back to stand over John.

"We've been imprisoned till now - there's a whole world outside!"

John smiled and nodded.

When Paul told him about his next party and reeled off the names John responded as if they were old friends, though with some the name was all he knew. Milly was coming and he grew excited.

Milly had made a decision to seem ignorant of any hurt. His response to her second phone call justified it. She'd discussed men acrimoniously with Marion and left it at that.

On the day of the party she was almost her old bouncy self. John had made no move to see her before it and the intervening time she'd occupied with dreaming and spending her savings. She bought a dark dress that made her look older and gave her skin and hair a lustrous look - she wanted her plump body to look less accessible. She tried so many perfumes on the back of her hand they numbed her sense of smell and she ended up choosing by name. The whole of Saturday was given up to preparation.

13

John and Milly were on easy terms as soon as they met. He passed from surprise to delight at being apparently irresistible to her. For the first half hour of the party he plied her with drinks, openly exhibiting his claim. It pleased her more than anything. He put his arm round her, chatted about this and that and wandered off greeting friends and strangers - it didn't matter which - exercising the amazing new confidence and warmth he'd acquired. Milly showed a sweet, almost withdrawing shyness towards everyone but himself, and his feeling of possession amounted almost to love. He was so caught up in it that when he asked her to leave and spend the night in a hotel and she shook her head he was almost content. The first spurt of disappointment was soaked up in dreams of what was to come. For the moment fantasy was even better.

They saw each other daily afterwards, Milly continuing to refuse in the manner of someone not able to risk her feelings so far again in case she were hurt. She gave in only when he was emotionally on his knees. For a few days John felt he'd never been so happy in his life - the same unanxious happiness as before - but as the week crept into a fortnight the other feelings came stealthily back - that the relationship was and could only be sexual and temporary. Sleeping together every night made him panic. He couldn't just leave - she was so totally involved. In fact her own feelings and objectives had become mixed to the point where she couldn't tell the next move from the next emotion, everything had become need.

John had told her he had to go back to Birmingham on

Sunday, Paul was giving up his flat to find lodgings in London. Some understanding had to be reached quickly.

They went walking on Saturday afternoon which was unusually hot but fresh for late summer. The freshness made them walk further than they meant and they ended up exhausted sitting together on a tree stump in the middle of a field of cornstalks. John had gone into a deep depression and couldn't haul himself out. He'd started off with ideas for explaining himself that seemed plausible. The line was to have been that her irresistibility was the cause of his faithlessness to Win - but now it didn't look so much like flattering her as presenting himself as a selfish betrayer of two. He started breaking off stalks and dropping them and when Milly rested against him he moved out of reach, leaning for a pimpernel.

She roused herself, saw his back and put her hand on it. "What's the matter?"

He didn't answer.

"I'll be coming to Birmingham in a few days."

No comment.

"We can see a lot of each other till term starts, and when it does I'll travel up every weekend." She moved closer to lean her head on his back and wait. His stiffness frightened her and she stood up. His hair had fallen over his forehead as he stared at the red flower he was turning between finger and thumb. She couldn't see his face and put her hand under his chin lifting it.

"I know you've got to go back," she said, reassuring him, "don't worry about it." His silence drained her and she looked vacantly at the turning flower, refusing to accept that the deadness was towards her. Her silence was now forcing him to speak and he stood up, suddenly irritable.

"We've been happy this week, haven't we? "

174

"Yes - "

"Both of us, I mean."

Her momentarily puzzled look turned to painful understanding. Instantly released he rattled out comments and explanations she didn't hear, her rush of understanding carrying them away. When he finally looked at her tears were streaming down her face.

"Did Paul ever tell you about Winifred?" - he saw her fear flare - "she's the woman I'm going to marry." He stared at the swaying poplars at the side of the field. "I've been in love with her so long" - and the memory brought tears to his eyes - "we quarrelled and I thought it was over but I've had a letter " - his hoarse voice stopped and pressing his hands together in front of his mouth he added, "My feelings don't change."

Milly buried her face in her hands.

"You're so wonderful I almost forgot her."

Her shoulders were shaking. Glancing up suddenly she caught his frightened sidelong look that as it filled with the shame he wouldn't acknowledge seemed spiteful.

"I'm committed to her."

She stared hard, reading behind the words and despising him. If she pushed further he'd hurt her more.

He turned to start the walk home.

14

In the middle of the following week John had two replies to his job applications, one from Mearsham and Boreden, a bookshop off Charing Cross Road, and the other from the prep school. They both offered interviews. The tone of the letter from the school damaged his dream a little - the message was that the candidate would be allowed only second class rail fare and if he turned the job down would pay for himself.

He regained his enthusiasm by buying himself a charcoal suit that his mother described as deathly but he saw as "dedicated" and trying it out on the bookshop. It worked its magic, he was offered the job but found himself delaying acceptance. When explaining to his mother it became clear just how strong a hold the school had taken.

"What excuse did you make?" she asked.

"First thing that came into my head - a new development in your health might make us move to the coast."

It took a moment to sink in. In imagination he could make her health a convenient inconvenience, as if her fierce self-discipline and independence meant nothing. After a considerable pause her anger broke over the question of the job:

"You damned fool!" she shouted in his face - and paused, checking herself: "What do you expect to get from hanging round here?"

He was stunned at the ferocity. His own indignation rose slowly: "I just felt I didn't want it," and a faint glimmer of understanding made him put his hands tentatively on her shoulders as she stood with her back to him bracing herself against the table.

There'd been tension between them since his second return from Cambridge. As he turned to her now he saw the angry desolation in her face and said nervously, trying to make her smile, "The boss would have been a nightmare, he was so keen I shouldn't forget my place he wouldn't shake hands!"

"You'll be kow-towing to someone wherever you go," she said stiffly.

"I won't, you know!" - and he dropped back.

The tension between them was becoming too painful and she wanted to break it. Part of her wanted to say the relationship they'd known was over but that her need would build a new one whatever the circumstances - and another part, hurt and recoiling, wanted to push him further off.

"When you start, whatever job you take, you'll be a burden," she said, "because someone will be responsible for your mistakes. They're a small-minded lot and make you feel as uneasy and inadequate as they do." She looked hard at him. "You can't stay here forever."

Without aggression he said, "I'll take the next job that offers," and she nodded.

Walking down the lane that was the last lap of his journey to the school John came to a point where the hedges suddenly stopped and he could see past the bend to a large greystone house with a tarmacked approach that looked as if it might be the place. Its roof was gleaming in the sunlight and his excitement soared. He was right - it was all he'd dreamed. The work and the place would be everything - his life would be transformed.

The smell of polish when he pushed open the heavy doors added its extra suggestions of intimacy and the teeming life it was waiting for. Easy, purposeful, he looked for someone to meet him. Here he could achieve everything by just 'being' - it wasn't the formal teaching but the living contact that mattered. Halfway down the hall he saw a notice pinned to the door, 'Interviewees,' and his stomach turned.

He knocked. There was no answer so he went in. There were three chairs at the far end of the narrow room and he chose one. It was the store room or the overflow from it with shelves of papers and books on either side - it excited him further. Looking out of the open window behind him he saw a field of tussocky grass and rocks and he could smell the sea.

The door opened and he stood up smartly to face a tall man with greying hair contracting his gaze to take him in.

"I've only just realised," he said smiling. "Mister....?"

"Whittam, John Whittam." He offered his hand and it was given a short burst of shaking.

"We'll try not to keep you waiting too long. I'm Mr Appleyard." John looked with new interest - it was the headmaster. "You've about 20 minutes to look over the place if you'd like. Mr Johnson will show you round." He roared down the corridor, "Mr Johnson!" - the last syllable prolonged and rising.

An old man appeared from a door on the left pinching out a cigarette.

"Would you be good enough to show Mr Whittam round the school?"

As John passed his open door the stink of smoke made him look in. It was as small as a broom cupboard, full of his cleaning stuff but with a chair, and a kettle perched on a box. He wanted to speak but the man was already moving off and John ran to catch him up. Something in his walk stopped him coming abreast and he followed. The shiny seat of his trousers made him feel more at home. They were passing empty cloakrooms and going through a pair of swing doors, coming to the classrooms. John opened the door of one to see a neat little room with about twenty desks in it. He came away smiling and asking about the gymnasium and art room, but there weren't any.

The dormitories were upstairs and a room called The Den was the first to attract his attention. Large armchairs, low tables, a few papers and books - not what he'd expected. Visions from a documentary showing precocious youngsters chatting in plummy trebles from propped positions were criss-crossing his expectations. No evidence of fun and the raw energy he was looking for. He checked to see if he'd made a mistake:

"The kids' room?"

Johnson nodded and went downstairs, assuming John must be looking for the staffroom. Following, he found himself in a doorway that had been opened for him and trying to understand what he was looking at. It filled him with uneasiness. It wasn't the mess - that didn't matter - an air of neglect that was short on comfort could have been right. The uneasiness now mounting to panic was a continuation of the confusion he'd felt upstairs. He remembered offices he'd been in during the last few weeks. Their feeling of order, however superficial, was reassuring. The chaos in front of him, the dirty limp curtains, the half empty bottle of stinking milk that Johnson now removed added to the feeling of violation now taking the place of fear. Memories rose involuntarily of some of his old schoolmasters whose bad breath, bigotry and desperate evasions had given him some of his earliest experiences of contempt and hatred. They'd punished the energy and undisciplined curiosity that threatened their lack of it. They were the ones on whom the system had worked.

Desperate for a switch of response he told himself it was all up to him. He could make what he liked of it. He'd be teaching young children not fully trained - and holding on to the thought reached the waiting room fairly composed. It was a child's memory and bound to be wrong.

A small slight youth about his own age came in and sat down, giving him a nervous smile. John smiled reassuringly like a senior. The headmaster followed and told them the third candidate wouldn't be coming. John found himself searching his face but whatever questions he was asking, the answers weren't there.

"Come into my study now, Mr Whittam."

John followed him.

15

In accepting this job John felt his adult life had started. From now on his thoughts would be directed outside himself. Other people were important not for the impression you could make on them but for the extra experience of them. Freedom from preoccupation about himself and what he wanted or expected from life would transform him.

When he got back from Cornwall Mrs Whittam found herself talking to a cheerful young man with confident eyes and for a while it was irresistible.

"Everything's in the melting pot," he said. "Life's wonderful!" - and some of her anxieties were loosened from their perch.

He felt protective of his mother now he was leaving, promising long visits in the holidays. She was grateful for the thought. The thought of his departure took precedence over everything. She'd imagined she was fully prepared for it but found she hadn't started. It came to her forcibly for the first time that he constituted her entire contact with life and it made her defenceless against the painful yearning that seemed to get stronger the longer he stayed. She wasn't just alone but without purpose - she'd only been part of life through him. No-one, not even she, denied her relevance as a mother, and that role was over. In her other world of strained friendships and pretended concerns she'd never been easy. Her nature had given her little access to the springs of life and what she'd had was going.

After several almost sleepless nights she woke from a light doze one morning to find herself looking forward to the breakfast in bed John had promised. Her room and the white morning light were comforting and when he came with the tray and sat leaning over her legs while she ate she felt there were things to look forward to. He'd marry and have children - new sources she'd fight to keep in touch with. His hopeful face encouraged a reflection in her own.

"I'm delighted, my love," she said, "I'm glad about it all. It's not the job that matters, it's the launching out." Her hand was tightening on his and the undercurrent in her voice made him stand up to stretch and examine his side view in her mirror.

"Will you like to visit me in Tintagel?" he asked. "I've got two rooms and the landlady says I can have a zed bed if I want. Think of the walks we'll have, and the views!"

She did and felt momentarily ecstatic.

"You'll be so pleased with me, Mum - your independent, hardworking, right-thinking son!"

"I'm glad you're going to think right," she smiled at him.

"You know what I mean. I'm not going in blind - "but as he said it he felt he was - "I know the hazards. I'll make friends and could never get tired of the place."

She smiled again.

Suddenly perfectly frank with her he said, "If I can't have Winifred I'll find someone like her. We'll have children. - I love children and you'll be part of a new world."

Her face lit up at the echo of her thoughts. "Yes, my love."

John busied himself for the rest of the week partly on her behalf, partly gathering his things together. The little piles of books on the floor of his bedroom gave him heart and took hers away but she held on to what he'd said.

The rooms of his new flat smelt of polish and of the roses the landlady had placed in the sunshine on the window ledge. He unpacked and looked round deciding where to put his pictures and books when they arrived. The place was attractive - the world outside even more so and he wanted to be in it. He met the landlady at the foot of the stairs.

"Everything all right, Mr Whittam?"

"Wonderful, wonderful," he said. She looked pleased. He rested his hand on the dark stair rail and looked at her bright face. "Thank you for the roses, they're magical."

She blushed. "Ah, you noticed. Some of my young men prefer no intrusions, not even by way of a bowl of flowers." She stood in the sunny hallway where the back and front doors were open. Over her shoulder he could see a garden - neat grass and tangled, bushy, brilliant flowers. "Would you like me to cook Sunday dinner for you? I do it for Mr Jones."

"That would be nice!"

She put a plump finger on his arm for an instant and tapped it. "You'll be wanting a breath of fresh air after all that travelling, and I have jobs to do. Let me know if there's anything you want." And she went down the hall into the garden.

John was disappointed, he wanted her there longer and to ask about Mr Jones. The later afternoon outside was heavy with heat bringing a sense of fatigue and sadness. He'd been carried for days on a wave of excitement he felt was dying and waited patiently for the walk to relax him but the unfamiliarity of the place demanded a response he was too tired to give.

He rested by a gate but it reminded him of his earlier visit. Desperate not to think along those lines he concentrated on the Jersey cows grazing in the distance and climbed over to get closer. They stood their ground, staring at him instead of breaking away. The unexpectedness of it startled and charmed him and he bagan calling in a gentle coaxing voice. He wanted to see if they'd move closer out of curiosity. They listened and watched with large brown curious eyes, unafraid. He'd got so close the smell of fur and dung began to overpower him but he was captured by their profiles, fine and sensitive as horses'. He'd never seen such beautiful cows and wandered among them. One or two leapt back startled and startling him. One let her bony skin-stretched head be patted but snatched it away again wetting his hand with her nose. He stood still watching. After a while when he gave them nothing and didn't move they tired of him, drifting away and letting out steaming strong-smelling dung a foot or two from his feet, wrenching grass in contemptuous mouthfuls. He watched their haunches and swaying tails retreating and felt deserted.

The first few weeks of term were deceptively easy. He learnt how to deal with the boys by observation - picking up manner and tone from what he saw going on in the corridor and a little from the headmaster's subtly self-glorifying technique in morning prayers. The trained responses of the boys helped. He'd been given a series of books for everything which he relied on to the letter and treated the children's different personalities with the businesslike but goodnatured indifference he saw around him. The boys saw he was abstracted and unmoved by them and that they could rely on a certain amount of good humour. They behaved accordingly and went about their work and their own pleasures hoping their paths wouldn't cross. An instantly relaxed relationship with a new master was a treat and his newness satisfied their curiosity for a time.

His original reaction to the staffroom had gone. The place seemed to have changed since term began. He didn't see much of his colleagues - he had only a couple of free periods and there was something in their manner that put off small talk. They were all overworked. He used the staffroom as a waitingroom, stuck strictly to what was expected of him and left and arrived on the dot of the appointed times. He took to cycling home for lunch in his flat, enjoying a brief chat and cup of coffee with the landlady who already treated him as her favourite.

His inner disengagement from pupils and staff alike made the first weeks look successful, but he began to get uneasy and bored. Afraid to rock the boat he put up with the boredom but it showed up in increasing irritability with the boys. Over the weekends he occasionally did so much cycling and walking that he spent Mondays in a trance and eventually decided to start on the intensive study of teaching methods he'd originally planned. It was time to find the most rewarding ones and develop a closer relationship with his classes.

16

Milly was hot in the train - her legs were impaled by the stiff hairs of the seat and her hands sticky. She opened the top panel of the window as far as it would go and raised herself up to gulp air but found herself choking on it. She slumped back disgruntled, stared at the woman opposite who was fidgetting with some fluttering hairs under her hat and relieved her boredom by studying her scaly-looking fingers and worn wedding ring. She had a boney face with no expression, it kept Milly's critical glance till the eyes gave a flick of peevishness. Smart, though, she conceded - correct shape in correct clothes. She became aware of her own sprawling legs and sat up. Wonder if she had any children? Maybe they'd grown up. She felt a spasm of joy at the child she was carrying and put her hand on her stomach. Nothing else mattered.

In spite of Marion's lugubrious face and ominous remarks when she heard, Milly had been joyous and triumphant from the start. She'd been through a later phase of uncertainty but it hadn't lasted. Nevertheless, the smile as she looked out of the window faltered. It was unfair. The journey to John shouldn't be spoilt by even a touch of anxiety. As if fear of the birth weren't enough! She was still angry with him but pushed it aside feeling she knew him better than he knew himself. Their last meeting only meant that at the time she'd had no means of holding him. She trusted in his fear of life as much as his responsiveness - her manoeuvres depended on both. The real obstacle had been removed - Winifred was out of it, she'd checked with Paul when she asked for John's address.

The train was due to arrive at three. Having decided

she'd be a fool to prepare him, she'd told John nothing, not even that she was coming. In her optimistic mood she hoped the sudden confrontation would surprise him into realising how much he cared for her. His evasions were playground stuff - what you'd expect till reality took a hand, and she had her hand lovingly over the reality. The outcome was assured because John had nothing to match her resources. Need was her greatest strength and she waited impatiently for it to be put to the test.

Stepping on to the platform alone was a shock - she was the only one getting off. She had to sit on a bench to collect herself, feeling suddenly afraid of everything - only the posters were old friends. There was too much space. Countryside stretched as far as she could see and the open station was so quiet she could hear birds singing. Even the air was different - keener. She got up, heaving her bags out of the station to find a taxi and be on her way.

The car parked at the exit had a couple of wooden boxes full of eggs on the back seat. She looked back feeling desperate and saw a head at one of the windows watching her. It disappeared and emerged with its body clothed in corduroy jacket and trousers.

"Can I help?" His gentle musical accent made her feel better.

"I was wondering if there was a taxi."

He smiled. "I'll take you where you want to go." She was surprised and hesitated. "Won't be the first time," he added, "make yourself comfy in the back," and he opened the door, pushed the boxes over and dusted the seat with his sleeve. "All right, me 'andsome?"

It took a second to work out it meant no more than "ducks" or "love" and she settled in. There were smells in the back, strong and clinging. The farmer was coming alongside with arms full of sacks of something bulky but light - she was relieved to feel the boot spring back but her eyes suddenly filled with tears at the thought she'd smell like a farmyard when she met John.

"Where d'you want to go?" he said, getting in.

"A Mrs. Merton's, I've got the address somewhere..." She was fiddling in her bag.

"I know where she lives - you a relative?"

"No."

"Visiting one of the lodgers?"

"Yes."

He grinned and started the car. "Your young man?"

"Yes." She found herself blushing.

"Serious?"

"Yes."

"That's the ticket." He whistled for a bit, lingering on the top notes. "Work at that posh school, does 'e?"

"Yes."

The whistling grew louder and shriller and she couldn't think. Fear of the space came back. Even the fields were empty. The light and the flashing hedges bothered her eyes and she looked straight ahead to see they were rounding a bend and slowing down at the sprinkling of houses that had come into view. The car stopped at the first.

"Here we are then."

She felt like crying. "Thank you" - but it wasn't enough - "Thank you very much!".

"My pleasure, m'dear," he said, helping her out, and before she could get her bags off the ground the door had slammed and he was off.

She stared at the house in front of her - it looked friendly. The paint was bright and the curtains pretty. Mrs Merton opened the door promptly and Milly, afraid of rebuff, explained clearly and coolly she was a friend of Mr Whittam's and had called to see him. The landlady glanced at her bags and asked if she'd like to wait in his room. Milly's face relaxed.

"He got in a few minutes ago - he's taking a walk," she said kindly and led her upstairs to his room.

Left to herself Milly sighed with relief - she'd made it - better still, he was out and she'd be in possession when he got back. She took off her coat and flung it over the back of a chair. "Home!" Her cheeks began to burn with excitement. Would he be excited to see her? It didn't matter. She sat in one of the chairs but leapt up again, going to the mantlepiece to finger the pencils and books on it. She turned to take in the room. In the conflict of love and fear she was cross again. No place for her, no thought for her, no memento. She swept the things to one end of the mantlepiece and put her handbag in the space but hearing swift, heavy steps on the stairs moved behind a chair, trembling and facing the opening door.

For a moment John refused to recognise the newly-frizzed head. He stood with his hand on the handle smiling vacuously.

"Hello," she said. A hot painful blush was burning her face and dazing her eyes and a new expression followed it. "How good it is to see you!" she said rushing towards him and burying her face in his chest. "Forgive me, forgive me - I had to come!" She looked up to see his face still vacant but pale. "I'm afraid and lonely. Nowhere to go but you. Be kind to me."

He put his arms round her as if a button had been pressed and moved her into the room closing the door. "What's wrong?" he said when he'd seated her.

Milly gave way to sobs of fear.

"Don't -" and the constrained tenderness gave her some relief - "it can't be as bad as all that."

She smiled at him and saw fear in his face but it seemed not so much of her as of himself. It was almost over then. She told him about the child and flung her arms round his waist drawing him closer, soaking his shirt front with tears and claiming him in a passion of gratitude that felt to him like consuming love.

Their marriage followed in a few weeks at a Registry Office in Wadebridge and was celebrated at Mrs Merton's. She'd been delighted and offered the use of her large drawing room where she filled every corner and shelf with flowers and helped with the baking. The room looked like a harvest festival and the cake stood alone on a table, surrounded by flowers.

Milly Whittam felt radiant. She'd been living in a dream and hadn't come out of it. Her heart sang when her mother's eyes looked up at John with respect - was there even a touch of envy?

Marion had at the last minute come to the Registry Office unexpectedly. Better nature or the final goadings of curiosity got the better of her. Her own affaiirs hadn't advanced in any direction but perhaps they'd be stimulated to make a move. If she'd hoped to see a restrained and awkward marriage she was disappointed. The light of achievement in Milly's eyes - the direct glance, confident expression and coyly managerial tone in addressing her husband - were hard to bear but she managed it and such a genuine affection emerged for her friend it surprised her.

There was only one unconquered spirit. Mrs Whittam had come to the ceremony and behaved towards Milly with courtesy and consideration but Milly felt her chances of winning her respect or affection were small. Happily she wasn't the girl to let it worry her. She could remain a stranger if that's what she wanted and she shrewdly assessed the mother's indifference extended in a different and perhaps more final way to her son. There was no contempt in her manner - even a degree of bitter relief.

For John his mother's reaction was difficult to understand. He'd not realised how much he worried about her opinion. He'd explained how the marriage had come about and how positively he'd come to feel about it and how warmhearted and affectionate his wife was. His mother had nodded, smiling as if he'd been telling her about a neighbour. She wondered why he wanted her approval. For a while her faith in him or rather in her understanding of him had vanished. This hasty enforced marriage and his touching hope it would turn out right in the end made her feel she'd reared a stranger.

The feeling of uneasiness his mother created got its counterbalance when Paul arrived flamboyantly dressed in grey suit and gilt-buttoned waistcoat and heartily approving of everything. He said he was proud of the part he'd played in it. Mrs Whittam heard from a distance his condemnation of Winifred - saw him eyeing Milly's plump figure and heard him comment, "Just what the doctor ordered." John, looking over to her once more for assurance and not getting it, turned back to Paul unreservedly grateful for him. He felt he was getting the nod from the masculine world.

17

Mrs Merton felt responsible for the wellbeing of the newlyweds and gave them her spare room at the top of the house as a bedroom - John's two rooms to be used as they thought fit. Strolling round her garden in the evening and hearing Milly clinking crockery or seeing John's light snap on over his desk warmed her. Part of her mind was perpetually engaged with them as if they'd been the children she hadn't had. She never interfered but the atmosphere of protection and warmth made them settle in as if it had been the home they'd planned.

John took to working in the evenings. He found the need for a rewarding way of teaching more urgent now his other needs were satisfied, and his notions of what this might involve had developed. He'd read a lot on teaching methods and was ready to put his interpretation into practice. His daily life with Milly at this stage seemed amazingly undemanding and having a child of his own gave the whole problem of education a serious turn. Without intending it he became a maverick in the staffroom - faintly disapproving and disapproved of and encouraged to stay out of the way. The classes saw a change of interest and perked up. For a while it did them good and John felt he was making progress of the sort he'd dreamed of.

It brought him to the position where he'd have liked to talk about it but there was only one member of staff that seemed accessible - a grey-haired, thin-faced maths master who'd answered his questions in the very early days and still gave him the occasional smile. To him John confided one day that he was pleased at the way things were going.

"Glad to hear it!" he said, looking up with strained eyes and returning to his marking. Thinking better of it he looked up again. "You've done well, I'd say. You don't seem to have any teething troubles. Some people are like that - born teachers. I can't say I was so lucky."

"How long have you been teaching?" John asked, pleased.

"About fifteen years - not all of them here, of course - I've been here six or seven. Before that I used to work in an office. In a way I'm a bit of an oddity - don't really belong with the Oxbridge lot. I started in a school where my external degree didn't matter so much - Appleyard must have been hard up when he let me in."

"You had an excellent degree, I heard," John said quickly.

"That helped, I suppose, but the teaching part came hard to me, though I never regretted it. I hated the office - it frightened me, it was all so meaningless. Teaching seemed a real job."

"It must have been hard reading for a degree in the evenings." John was looking at his yellow-white skin and its heavy lines.

"I suppose so but it became a form of escape. With maths the possibilities seemed limitless - the opposite to what I felt in my job."

John nodded.

"Of course, to a young man like yourself what I'm doing at fifty must seem the waste of a life - but not for me. For one thing I'm dealing, however simply, with a subject I enjoy and that never fails to exert a sort of magic over me." He looked questioningly at John, hoping he'd say something that would let him expand, but John had never been interested in maths and couldn't think what to ask.

"But you found teaching hard?" he said.

"For a time - but I love children, they're splendid creatures - honestly themselves, nice or nasty."

"But not in their work" - John's interest leaping at finding the opening he'd hoped for - "I've been getting them to write poetry and it comes out imitating everything they've read. It's hard to get them to do anything else, but the other day something real came on my desk - like to see it?"

Arthur Baker looked at his watch. "I'd like to, but I've got to mark that lot by twelve."

"Of course," John said, going to fetch the poem.

Baker read it, smiled, nodded and put it down. "I think I see what you mean," he said and stretched his hand towards the pile of books.

"Do you really like it?" John insisted before the first cover was open. "What do you think of the drawing at the top?" The title was *A Cat with a Mouth like That* and under it a brutal drawing of a cat with cavernous mouth and milk bottles for teeth.

"Amusing,," Arthur said.

"You don't know how different it is from what I've been getting. It made my week."

Arthur nodded and took another book, having ticked and crossed his way through the first. At the bottom of the page he looked up again. "I can give you a tip if you like," he said, staring shyly, his voice hesitant. "If you waken a sense of adventure in the subject slowly they'll find there's room for all their different responses. Some might find a genuine interest in it."

John blushed. Hadn't he been saying that?

"I mean," Arthur went on, "they'll follow any new fashion if the teacher sells it hard enough. To start with they'll just be showing off. The thing is to make them feel the subject's magic." He crossed his legs and doodled around an ink stain on his trousers.

"But that's what I'm trying to do," John said, hurt. "I've worked out interesting experiments and given them unusual things to do. If I can't infect them with my own enthusiasm how can anything get done?"

"I don't know" - Arthur sounded hesitant - "but it won't happen by being an inspired ringmaster. If you teach them new tricks their interests will die when you leave, or before then." He looked up. "I don't know how English is best taught but I know a little about kids. You mustn't take offence" - he looked unhappy - "I would have liked to talk to someone when I started, and I was much older than you."

"Of course I couldn't take offence" - repressed irritation was making John's answer explosive - "I value your experience, but why do you think I'm a ringmaster?"

"Why, of course I don't! I'm just warning you against it. It's a bad mistake if you want real returns. It's a good technique for promotion though - looks good from the outside."

Even more offended, John persisted out of the need to understand: "Well, how do I go about awakening their curiosity?"

The defiant scepticism made Arthur put his hand on John's arm. "Now how do I tell you that, my boy?" he smiled, "You can't pick up that in a day. You'll only get it by trial and error. I'm still working at it. The only thing I can tell you is you must be patient: patient interest in them more than their work. Don't always be interested in those who seem to be the best - sometimes the best are hidden. You can't do it by teaching the whole class at once - work with small groups. Chat to them about this and that and let them see you find them interesting and the subject interesting.

194

Don't push too much, don't make them feel they've got to show off. Enjoy the slow pace of the slowest. It may not seem easy while you're excited but when it begins to work the rewards are enormous."

John was touched, confused and angry and let Arthur get back to his marking. Later, thinking it over, he wondered if that quiet, friendly, unnoticeable man was a good teacher. He looked worn out. Was exhaustion part of the reward? At some points Arthur's idea of teaching was a travesty of his own. How many years did you have to wait to know if it worked? How did you feed your own excitement? Surely your own enthusiasm was enough - excitement was infectious. What Arthur said sounded like abandoning all ambition. Was he supposed to turn himself on like a tap and not bother where it went? The kids were interesting but not that interesting.

His first attempt to chat felt like a failure. Arthur had admitted he wasn't a high-flier and John felt the need of another viewpoint. He decided to try again with Derek Jones, who after all was staying in the same house. He'd already made one or two unsuccessful attempts to strike up conversation on the stairs but, since his marriage, hadn't bothered. Derek responded to "Good morning" as if it were a culture shock but was reputed to be in the fast lane for promotion. He taught classics, a subject that seemed to be in good odour with the head, and had a great deal to say in the general running of the school. John had seen him come away flushed with pleasure after a conversation with Appleyard - as if he'd been scaling the heights - perhaps because whenever there were problems of organisation he was asked for his opinion. In the classroom he was an autocrat more terrifying to the boys than the headmaster.

John wondered if his own view of teaching lay somewhere between Arthur's and Derek's.

He watched him in the staffroom one afternoon come silently to his chair, pull it out and sit with such precision that this basic act looked like a pleasure or an achievement. He drew his hand firmly over a set of exercise books and leaned for his pen. Perhaps he was really a nervous man and every act had to have the sanction of ritual. Keeping an open mind John went through with his plan to ask him in for a drink on Saturday.

Milly was feeling particularly low-spirited that day.

"What d'you invite him for?" she said when John came to help in the kitchen.

He thought for a moment. "He lives in the same house, we work together."

"Not good enough!"

John put his arms round her waist.

"Nobody's invited us. Absolutely nobody!"

"That's different. They probably think we want to be left alone for a bit."

"Hmph!" She opened a tin and arranged some cakes on a plate. "Well, I'm not going to entertain him for long, I get tired. I'll go to bed at quarter to ten whether he's here or not." A few seconds later: "Couldn't you have asked me first?"

"Put your feet up - he'll understand."

Later, when she was dressing, she started again. John was sitting on the bed and she was looking at her large belly in the mirror. "What's he like to talk to?"

"Very self-centred - but then he's a bachelor. I don't know anything about him really, that's why I asked him."

"Does he do well at school?" She came to sit by him and

put on some low-heeled furry slippers that might tell Jones something if he bothered to look.

"Seems to. The boys are afraid of him. I suppose he teaches quite well. Obviously looking for promotion."

"That'll be you soon," she said, sounding excited.

"Give us a chance! I've only just started." He swivelled his socked feet on to the bed and looked pleased at her motherly appearance.

"You won't want to teach forever, with your brains" - tapping him dismissively on the head.

"Why not? - you do."

"I'll teach till I've got a bigger family, but I want something better for you." She turned, expecting him to smile at her confidence but his expression wasn't pleased.

"You've got to understand" - slippping into his classroom manner - "I take the job I'm doing seriously."

"You might want to go on doing it, then?"

"Perhaps." There was a pause.

"I don't believe it."

He looked cross. For some reason he'd appointed himself guardian of principle in this relationship - especially when it involved doing as he liked. So far she'd let him get away with it. Now she put her hand gently on the thin neck she liked stroking and he felt uneasy. "Let's get something straight," he said, "I can't work if I'm not interested, so it's no good getting ideas about fancy jobs."

"What's Jones coming for if you're not curious about getting on? He's no bundle of fun!"

He was silent. "I need to talk to someone about teaching."

"Shouldn't think he knows much about it - not his main interest." She was touching up her hair and confidently added, "He'll be no help, might make you feel worse. If you

197

question him he'll probably look at you as if you're wet - his view will be you've either got it or you haven't."

John had a dismal feeling she was right. In a sudden reversal of feeling towards her he said, "Their eyes brighten up when I come in - I must be doing something right. They almost all wrote something like a poem last week - something spontaneous."

She was pleating the hem of her dress with her fingers. When she answered it was distantly: "You're enjoying it now but it won't go on forever. I was thinking about the future."

"Don't you see," he pleaded, "it's for the future - theirs - mine - confidence in our own responses."

She looked vague - perhaps bored. In the clinches, she thought, it always came down to the same thing -survival. "You'll get too tired to keep that up all the time," she said, and after a pause: "We're different, you and me. I like the kids all right as they are - you want too much."

Depressed and shocked, he was so unnerved that his curiosity had disappeared by the time Jones arrived. They made a submissive audience for Jones's anecdotes about his career to date - and he really enjoyed his evening.

18

Both attempts to talk had set up anxieties he'd never expected. It didn't mean he hadn't a place in school-teaching but it did mean he'd have to find his own on his own. For the first time he felt out on a limb. When he got back to his classes he'd lost some of his confidence and was uncertain about the kind of energy he was putting into them. For a time he put in less and instead became increasingly preoccupied with Milly's pregnancy. It replaced some of the excitement he'd lost. She let him fuss over her - queened it and relaxed. Occasionally she was slightly irritated at something in his stare that made her feel she was only the container, but it quickly disappeared. When she told him to put his hand on her stomach and feel the kicking she was delighted at his awed amazement and happier than she'd ever been. This lasted till just before the birth.

Then she became entirely preoccupied with the birth itself. Fantasies faded as the day approached and the more anxious she grew the crosser she became with a devotion that seemed to have less and less bearing on the real situation. To keep her calm he made little of her fears and she felt it was lack of interest in anything but the outcome. He was still preoccupied with the dream but attempted a more personal and compassionate understanding - it made her worse - she felt the insult of the effort.

John submitted to it all. He'd read the right books and been warned.

Alongside the dream and helping promote it was a steady deterioration in his relationship with his classes, especially his own form. The sureness of footing had never come back. It was leading to repressive rule. He'd tried to slip back into orthodox methods but dull lessons were only tolerable if you'd never expected anything else or if there was a hard hand backing them. His class's biggest disappointment was that they felt they were no longer interesting to him. When repression took over completely they grew furious. Even new tricks of mischief only reclaimed his attention in part - but they knew they were on the right track.

He'd pretended to ignore too much in the early stages of alienation, while letting them see him white and drawn with the corners of his mouth twitching. For a while they hadn't understood why he didn't retaliate - then suddenly, violently and indiscriminately he started cuffing and shouting. One boy was left with the red imprint of a hand on his white face for an entire lesson. For a short time they were subdued. Then the real battle began.

He opened the classroom door one morning to an unnerving silence. Searching their faces he saw their eyes bright and excited. One of them, head hung down, arms folded, was shaking with suppressed laughter. The boy behind kicked his seat sharply and he sat up and stared ahead like the rest. John walked to his desk feeling their eyes rake over him for purchase points. He put his case down and pulled out the drawer for paper, taking out a sheaf and beckoning to a boy in the front row to give it out:

"A sheet each."

The boy took it and walked between the rows handing it out while the faces on either side broke into smiles like silvery undersides of leaves in a gust.

John felt drained. Drawing his lips together in a thin line of disapproval he directed it against them and walked between the rows of desks with his hands behind him. A head in front of him turned suddenly, making excited eye-communications with the boy opposite and he clamped his hand over it like a vice, turning it. When he'd passed the pale face contorted with wild silent laughter. At one of the front desks John stopped a moment, surprised to see a boy's hand raised.

"Please sir, my pen makes blots, sir. Can I do it in pencil?"

"Do what in pencil?"

"Whatever we're going to do."

"Sit quiet till you're told." And he forced the hand down.

During the interchange the boy on the other side of the gangway slipped something into one of John's baggy pockets. There was a small explosion of glee from the class. John turned to face it.

"That's enough! I'll have complete silence. I don't know what's got into you but I'm warning you -" He felt a faint pressure against his hip. There was a unanimous scream of delight as he looked down to see his pocket changing shape. A bulge at one end suddenly disappeared. He put his hand in and with a shout of terror flung a small grass snake to the other side of the room.

The screeching, shouting, rocking mass filled him with panic. One boy was moving towards the coiled heap near the wall.

"Oh sir, you've hurt it! It wouldn't do you any harm."

John pounced on him, holding him so fiercely he winced. "Is that your snake?" he shouted. The boy, white as paper, couldn't answer. John shook him furiously and when he'd finished the child, trembling from head to foot, burst into tears.

Several voices called out: "He didn't do it, sir!"

"Was it your snake?" John shouted again.

"Yes."

"Pick it up! Don't dare - don't ever dare to bring such a thing into the classroom again."

The boy picked up the limp snake, carrying it gently in his hands back to his seat, crying and wiping his eyes and nose on his blazer sleeve. The class looked at John with reproachful hatred. The boldest of them said again, "It wasn't him - he didn't put it in your pocket," but John's fury had suddenly left him and he looked at the boy blankly. When he picked up his chalk he saw his hand trembling.

"You're behaving like..." His voice was wavering and he couldn't control it. Resting both hands on his desk and looking over their heads at the far wall he waited till he was calmer. "We were going out," he said "to write a description of whatever took your interest," and after a pause: "Now you can use the paper for a spelling test. Take out your pens."

From this point the terms were set. Their sense of power reinforced by a new righteousness and the danger of expressing it gave them what they needed. This was an expression of real life their spirits understood. Before, their knees cramped under desks, skins smelling of sweat and ink, they'd looked out of the windows with longing or thrown the occasional pellet. Now interest flared like dry grass whenever John entered the room.

If he attempted to conduct a poetry lesson in the old way there was chaos. They answered his questions with crude stupidity or deliberate contempt, eyes flickering to the grinning faces around them, gathering support. When he asked them to write poems they wrote wild, idiotic or obscene verse. Sometimes they wrote lampoons against John, very crudely and childishly disguised but disguised enough to give them the confidence to parade their innocence if challenged.

It was useless walking between the desks reseating vagrant boys and speaking in low calm tones barely concealing his rage and panic - worse than useless shouting at them and hitting as he had done when it first dawned on him this was how it was going to be. He felt it was a fight to the death - his. Their blazing pack-energy overmatched his pale flame of converted fear to the point where he thought of letting them take over without a struggle, for the peace of being sacked for incompetence.

The strain had an effect on his health and appearance. Every day he developed excruciating headaches and the slightest noise or disorder intensified the pain. His colleagues noticed enough to ask him if he were ill and eventually even the children began to be uneasy at the spectacle of their power translated into his ill-health. They didn't really want that. For the first time in weeks his humanity became real to them and it took the joy out of the fight. Underneath it all they still wanted him to be on their side and work with them as he had before, and there grew up a faintly contemptuous compassion for him that expressed itself in little gifts from the worst offenders. They half hoped he'd return and take over.

When John's child was born he was only a little disappointed to hear it was a boy.

Milly's ward was a small one and she had a bed in a corner. She watched men walking in confidently towards their wives - smiling, holding flowers and parcels - and he came in last, pale and empty-handed. She flushed with shame at his thin, weakened, bent-shouldered height. Why couldn't he come in striding like the rest? She glanced round at the women she'd struck up a friendship with - only temporary but vivid because of the intensity of the experience they'd shared. They were taking stock with that fraction of their attention set aside for it and Milly would have to put up with their diplomatic comments later.

John kissed her pale face and smiled into her darkened, dark-shadowed eyes. She looked intensely irritable.

"How are you, darling?" he said, sitting on the edge of the bed.

"You're not allowed to sit on the bed," she said, pushing his thigh fiercely, "what do you think the chairs are for?"

He sat down by the side of her. "Where's our son?"

"They're bringing them out in a minute." At a time like this he still wasn't connecting - 'our son' - pompous ass!

Feeling her hatred he looked at her carefully and remembered what she'd been through. "What was it like, Milly? Was it a good birth?" He was trying to lay hold of her emotional state and put his hand on hers, looking with a concern that half justified her interpretation of 'fake'. It frightened her. She was always catching him in the act of composition. If he had to do it over an issue like this, what was left for them?

"What a damned silly question!" she said "Ask any of these women if it was a good birth. You have one!"

He saw her fear and exhaustion and felt overcome with pity. "My love, I'm sorry - I didn't mean that." There was something real in his voice that appeased her.

"It was worse than most," she said, "it lasted so long, he just wouldn't be born."

John looked pained. "The boy's all right?" he asked suddenly .

Irritation flashed in her face. "He's all right - a bit blue, but all right. It's me he tore up."

The babies were coming in and cots unfolded and placed neatly by each bed. John stared with disbelief at the wrinkled, fiercely featured creature swathed in a cotton sheet- very black hair, face going red but with a touch of blue, features painfully distinct with a nose and chin so large they looked clumsy on so small a head, as if the beginnings of function and character were hurting him. Completely absorbed he moved to touch him and Milly took his hand.

"Leave him, you mustn't pick him up." She was mollified by his genuineness. "Most fathers are too scared anyway."

The next few weeks Milly felt she was convalescing. Her mother came to stay and she struck up an intimacy with her she hadn't known since childhood. Suddenly they were on the same side again - intimate, affectionate, exclusive. John felt displaced. Milly's mother did all the cooking and housework and supervised her daughter's handling of the baby but in that were the seeds of estrangement. Feeling stronger each week she got annoyed at minor infringements of her rights like the snatching of pins from her hand when she was fumbling with a nappy. She bagan to feel the place was crowded. A few days afterwards her mother went home.

Now John was allowed to give full rein to his devotion. Fussy and anxious, he was worse than her mother.

"How long did you soak the bottle? It says at least three hours."

"Don't fuss - who feeds and looks after him when you're at school?"

Whenever he could he bathed him, saying Milly was too fierce with the towel. When Simon woke in the night Milly nudged John and feeling the job would be done more tenderly by him he got up. He'd been dismayed she couldn't breast-feed him and thinking the boy was being deprived hugged him to his bony breast to make it up to him.

When Milly wasn't taking full advantage of his willingness she found the intensity of concern puzzling. For the time being she was grateful and content to let it rest as proof of his family-centredness.

19

John was preparing barricades of work for his classes before the Autumn term began and was hard at it when Mrs Merton knocked one evening to tell him he had a phone call. He went downstairs tense and tired but within seconds Milly heard his excited voice floating back up. She looked over the bannisters and saw him running his fingers over the old mirror in front of him.

"Guess who that was!" he said, running up to her.

"Who?"

"Paul! You'll never guess what he said. Wait a minute - I've got to sit - can't stop my heart thumping - this is ridiculous." Milly shut the door and waited. "He's offered me a job - I mean a good job - with him in his uncle's firm." He stared at her wide-eyed as if he'd said it all.

"Doing what?" she asked, thinking he'd never tell her.

"Don't know yet. I just said yes - " grinning as if nothing else mattered - "the firm collects newspaper clippings for celebrities, I know that much, and I think it's branched out into other things this year. Newish business doing amazingly well. Sort of personnel job, I think - said I'd be perfect for it, but I'll find out more when I go up on Saturday."

"Where?"

"London."

"Oh God, how wonderful!" A memory of hectic energy, packed streets and distraction and titillation in every shop window dazed her mind like alcohol. She came to. "How much would you get?"

"A hundred a month more than here!"

She rolled up her eyes and pink with pleasure went to

sit on his knee. John hugged her close. She fondled his hair, saying what a puzzle he was and how she'd always known what he was cut out for - success. She didn't say any more in case he back-tracked. She asked the pressing question indirectly:

"Was Paul amazed how quickly you agreed?"

"I don't think it crossed his mind I'd refuse. I'm not home and dry yet though, I've got to meet the uncle. Paul says it's a formality."

She pictured John in expensive suits and beautifully tailored shirts with a dash of daring in colour or cut and looked at his sensitive fingers remembering how their delicacy had fascinated her at Paul's party when they'd met. A job like that would be all parties! He'd look as he had then, sophisticated and distinguished.

For the next few days everything they did was transformed. Everything came easy. Waking up for Simon in the night didn't tire them. They became intimate in a way they'd never been and Milly's bright plump face looked into John's with the love and admiration he felt he'd waited his life for. A few months ago he'd have seen the job as so limited as to be feared and now it had expanded his life beyond recognition. A place among adults in an adult world felt like life and the opportunities to meet exciting people a bonus he'd never dreamed of. Milly'd take up teaching when they'd had their family - she'd be so much better at it and he'd enjoy it through her.

On Saturday John, emanating a power and confidence that made the outcome a certainty, went to his interview. Milly couldn't wait at home. Wrapping Simon against the wind she walked to the bus stop to catch the only bus to town. With him bundled against her she felt she could face anything. The Cornish sea still repelled her but today she could look at it - not for long! - and the looking out of one window suggested looking into others. Dreams took over.

Getting off the bus in the small seaport brought her back. The reality of the place hurt. Shops packed together in a small space, narrow crowded streets with the intensiveness scattered by infinite daylight and clear air, the unending space that made her tense. The locals moved slowly, talking in groups. Shopkeepers were so slow she felt frenzied - their eyes sharp with inquisitiveness.

There were a few tourists around still and in them she found what she was looking for. The self-conscious faces of a chilly group standing outside a restaurant drew her to them. Dressed emphatically for summer and pleasure they seemed disappointed of both and looked irritable. She listened at a safe distance. The adolescent son and daughter wanted pasties on the beach, the parents comfort inside. They looked exposed to more than cold. The adult male used the weight of his authority to push open the door and his shivering wife followed him in. Two sulking stiff-hipped adolescents waited for the door to swing back, then opened it for themselves.

Milly, touched and eased, looked down at Simon, wiped his mouth, pressed her cheek against him and followed.